BATTLE TESTED

LAURA SCOTT

HARLEQUIN® LOVE INSPIRED® SUSPENSE

Special thanks and acknowledgment are given to Laura Scott for her contribution to the Military K-9 Unit miniseries.

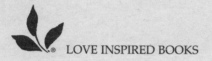

LOVE INSPIRED BOOKS

Recycling programs for this product may not exist in your area.

ISBN-13: 978-1-335-54403-2

Battle Tested

www.Harlequin.com

Printed in U.S.A.

The Lord is my rock, and my fortress, and my deliverer; my God, my strength, in whom I will trust; my buckler, and the horn of my salvation, and my high tower.
—*Psalms* 18:2

This book is dedicated to all the men and women who have served our country and have paid the ultimate price in order to protect our freedom.

ONE

Two fatal drug overdoses in the past week.

Exhausted from her thirteen-hour shift in the intensive care unit, First Lieutenant Vanessa Gomez made her way down the hallway of the Canyon Air Force Base hospital, grappling with the impact of this latest drug-related death.

The medication both young men had overdosed on, Tyraxal, had been touted as the best new drug on the market to treat PTSD. Of course, no meds were risk free, but she was troubled by these two recent deaths. Not just because her young brother, Aiden, also suffered from PTSD, although he wasn't on that particular medication as far as she knew, but because she'd heard Tyraxal was highly addictive and it seemed these recent overdoses proved it.

The corridor lights abruptly went out, enclosing her in complete darkness. She froze, instinctively searching for the nearest exit sign, when strong hands roughly grabbed her from behind, long fingers wrapping themselves around her throat.

The Red Rose Killer?

It had been months since she'd received the red rose indicating she was a target of convicted murderer and prison escapee Boyd Sullivan. She struggled against her attacker, wishing now that she'd brought Eagle, her protective attack Doberman, to work with her.

No! Dear God, please help me!

She kicked back at the man's shins, but her soft-soled nursing shoes didn't do much damage. She used her elbows, too, but couldn't make enough impact that way, either. Her phone was off, so she didn't bother digging it out of her bag. The attacker's fingers moved their position around her neck, as if searching for the proper pressure points.

"Why?" she asked in a harsh whisper as she tried to break his hold. She'd helped Boyd once after he'd gotten into a fight, tending to his wounds. So why was he intent on killing her? She clawed at his hands, but they were covered in plastic gloves.

"Because you're in my way…" the attacker said, his voice low and dripping with malice.

The pressure against her carotid arteries grew, making her dizzy and weak. Black spots dotted her vision.

She was going to die, and there was nothing she could do to stop it.

Poor Aiden, he'd be left all alone…

Her knees sagged, then she heard a man's voice. "Hey, what's going on?"

Her attacker abruptly let go just as the lights came on. She fell to the floor, wincing against the blinding brightness while struggling to breathe. The sound of pounding footsteps echoed along the corridor.

"Are you okay?" A man wearing battle-ready camo rushed over, dropping to his knees beside her. A soft, wet, furry nose pushed against her face and a sandpapery tongue licked her cheek.

"Yes," she managed, hoping he didn't notice how badly her hands were shaking.

"Stay, Tango," the stranger ordered. He ran toward the stairwell at the end of the hall, the one that her attacker must have used to escape.

"Hey, Tango," she whispered, stroking the golden retriever's soft coat and resting her forehead against his fur. He wasn't Eagle, her protective Doberman, but he was obviously well trained in offering comfort.

Hearing footsteps pounding in the stairwell, she quickly lifted her head and struggled to her feet. She slipped off her shoulder bag and wrapped the strap around her hand, the only thing she could use as a weapon in the event Boyd was coming back to finish the job.

The stairwell door opened revealing a tall, muscular man with wavy, sandy-brown hair. His expression was full of concern as he approached. "Sure you're all right?"

She nodded, her shoulders slumping in relief. "Yes. Did you see him? The man who attacked me?"

Her rescuer shook his head, his emerald green eyes heavy with remorse. "I'm sorry, but I didn't get a good look at him. Other than general statistics like medium height and build. He had a ski mask covering his head, so I can't even tell you his hair color."

Boyd Sullivan was medium height and build. Then again so were half the men on base.

But only Boyd Sullivan had sent her a red rose.

"Thank you." She drew in a deep breath, hoping to calm her racing heart. "I'm First Lieutenant Vanessa Gomez. I'm one of the ICU nurses here. I'm not sure what would have happened if you hadn't chosen that moment to come down this hallway."

"Captain Isaac Goddard," he said, introducing himself. "I'm glad I was here to help. Do you think this is related to Boyd Sullivan?"

Vanessa grimaced, gingerly palpating her tender neck. No doubt she'd have bruises tomorrow. "Unfortunately, yes. I believe my attacker is the Red Rose Killer."

"I'm sorry to hear that." Isaac's expression turned grim.

"Me, too." Although she still didn't understand Boyd's motive for wanting her dead after she'd gone out of her way to help him.

"You need to call this in to the Security Forces, specifically to my buddy Captain Blackwood," Isaac said. "There were rumors that Boyd was seen recently on base, but this attack on you proves it."

She nodded and dug in her bag for her cell phone. She powered it up, her fingers still trembling from the aftermath of her attack. Vanessa sometimes turned her cell phone off when she was working in the intensive care unit. Obviously, she should have turned it on the moment she'd left the ICU, although the attack had been so unexpected, she doubted the phone would have been any help.

She shivered and punched in Justin Blackwood's number. She had his contact information from the ad hoc investigative team that had been put together months ago when Boyd had first sent roses identifying his next targets. As she waited for him to pick up, she marveled at how Tango stood right between her and Isaac, as if willing to protect both of them.

Justin didn't answer so she left him a brief message about her attack and the likelihood that Boyd had found her, and she asked him to return the call.

"Call the cops," Isaac said. "They need to take your statement."

"I'd prefer to speak directly to Justin." Vanessa glanced up and down the empty hallway. "It's not as if there are any clues here for them to find. He was wearing gloves, so there's no point in dusting for prints."

He looked as if he wanted to argue, but asked, "Where are you headed?"

"Home." She slipped her phone into her bag. "What about you?"

He shrugged. "I was going to stop by and see if Lieutenant Colonel Flintman was around, but that can wait. Right now, I think it's best if I walk you home."

Normally Vanessa considered herself a strong, independent woman, more than capable of taking care of herself. She'd needed to be strong, especially for her younger brother, Aiden, who was having a rough time since returning to base four weeks ago after his latest six-month deployment. But this vicious attack at the hospital, a place she considered her second home and immune to this type of violence, had put a serious dent in her confidence. "I'd appreciate that, thanks."

"No problem." Isaac fell into step beside her. Tango stayed at Isaac's left side, and she wondered about the dog's role in Isaac's life.

She could guess, considering Isaac had been heading to Lieutenant Colonel Flintman's office. She'd left the doctor a message earlier that afternoon about her concern about Tyraxal. The kindly psychiatrist might have some information related to the medication, so she hoped he returned her call, soon.

Isaac might be seeing Lieutenant Colonel Flintman for the same reason Aiden did.

Not that it was any of her business.

They stood for a moment waiting for the elevator, and Isaac must have picked up on her curiosity because he gestured to the dog. "I don't think I introduced my therapy dog, Tango."

She belatedly noticed that Isaac sported a pair of gold wings on his collar indicating he was a pilot. She smiled at the animal. "Tango is an amazing dog, so calm and reassuring. He's obviously good at his job."

Isaac shrugged. "Yeah, he's a great dog, but while I appreciate having him around, my top priority is to bring home Beacon, the dog who saved my life in Afghanistan. Beacon belonged to my closest friend, and I've been working day and night to get him back. After all this time, he's finally due to arrive tomorrow."

Instinctively, she reached out to place her hand on his arm. "I heard about your efforts to bring Beacon home, and I'm so glad it's finally happening."

"Me, too." He covered her hand on his arm briefly and she found herself liking the warmth of his skin. Then he moved away when the elevator arrived, breaking the connection. He held his hand over the electronic eye until she was safely inside, then stepped in behind her.

She told herself her reaction to Isaac was nothing more than misplaced gratitude for the way he'd saved her life with his impeccable timing. Yet she couldn't help sending him a sidelong glance, appreciating his sandy-brown hair, chiseled features, clean-cut square jaw and bright green eyes. She glanced away, telling herself to knock it off.

Outside, the October air smelled of pine trees and morning glories. She loved autumn in east Texas; it was her favorite time of year.

"Lead the way," Isaac said, when they reached the street in front of the hospital.

"I live in a small two-bedroom house about eight blocks from here," she said, turning left and taking the road that went past the church and veterinary clinic. "My younger brother, Aiden, has been staying with me since his return from combat four weeks ago. He's on medical leave, suffering badly from PTSD, and I'm at a loss as to how to help him."

Isaac didn't say anything for a long moment, then he finally spoke. "I'm working through my own issues, so I understand what he's dealing with." Isaac glanced at her, his eyes shadowed by the darkness. "I hope you realize he has a long road to recovery ahead of him."

"I understand," Vanessa said softly. "He's doing everything right so far, attending therapy sessions with Lieutenant Colonel Flintman and taking his medication as ordered. Aiden is also on the list to get a therapy dog of his own, but the first attempt didn't go well, and a second one hasn't been made available to him yet."

"I'll talk to him, if you think it may help," Isaac offered.

Vanessa was humbled by his willingness to put himself out there on behalf of a stranger. "Thank you, Captain. I'd be grateful for anything you can offer."

"Sounds good. Maybe you can introduce me tonight, if he's around. And please, call me Isaac."

"If you'll call me Vanessa," she said with a smile. Despite her recent attack, she experienced a surge of hope. She was so grateful for Isaac's willingness to help her brother, she could have hugged him, but managed to restrain herself.

Maybe Isaac was just what Aiden needed to turn the corner on battling his illness.

Maybe this was exactly God's plan.

Isaac couldn't believe he'd actually told Vanessa about his PTSD, something he rarely talked about outside of therapy sessions. For the first time in weeks, he didn't feel the urge to hide the truth about what he was going through.

Maybe this meant he'd turned the corner on his healing process.

The sound of a car door slamming shut made Vanessa jump and nervously glance over her shoulder. He reached out to capture her hand in his, recognizing she was still suffering the aftermath of her attack.

"It's okay, you're safe with me," he assured her. Would she end up having nightmares as a result of the near strangulation? He hoped not. "Tell me about Boyd Sullivan and why he wants to hurt you."

She grimaced and shook her head. "Nothing to tell."

Isaac chose his words carefully. "Vanessa, I know firsthand that talking through an event is better than keeping it bottled inside. And I'm willing to listen without passing any judgment."

They took several steps heading west on Webster Street, past Canyon Drive, where most of the base housing was located, before she let out a heavy sigh. "There really isn't anything to the story. Boyd holds a grudge against the Air Force for dishonorably discharging him and he's coming after people who he believes are responsible for his downfall."

He'd heard the same theories. The base had been on high alert for months now, and apparently with good reason. Sullivan was getting bold and impatient, judging by the way he'd sneaked into the hospital to attack Vanessa.

He cast a glance her way. She was beautiful, her long dark hair pulled back in a ponytail, matching her chocolate-brown eyes. Beside him, she was petite in her pale blue scrubs covered by a white scrub jacket. Her honeysuckle scent made him think of home, and he was glad he'd been in the right place at the right time for once.

"And what about you? Did he want a personal relationship with you?" he guessed.

"Not at all," Vanessa quickly denied. "In fact, I helped him one night while he was still in basic training, providing medical care for wounds he'd suffered as a result of a barroom brawl. He didn't want to go to the ER and get in trouble, so I provided first aid from the kit I carry in my car. That's why this attack doesn't make any sense."

She paused, then added, "He told me that I was the first person to be nice to him without expecting anything in return. Does that sound like a rational reason to want me dead?"

"No, it doesn't," he agreed. "I wonder if he thought your being nice to him meant you were interested in something more." To be honest, Isaac couldn't imagine any red-blooded man not being attracted to Vanessa.

He was attracted to her. Not that he was going to do anything about it. He let go of her hand, reminding himself that he wasn't interested in another relationship. Been there, done that, didn't work out, end of story.

In his experience women thought they could help a guy get over his issues, yet when they learned they couldn't, they decided the guy wasn't worth the trouble and moved on.

And maybe he wasn't worth the trouble. He couldn't blame Amber for leaving him when his panic attacks prevented him from leading a normal life. He especially didn't appreciate her hovering over him. He used to think he'd get better and move on with his life, but he now understood PTSD didn't ever go away. There were strategies to deal with it, sure, but it wasn't like being treated for an infection that would be cured by a course of antibiotics.

No, this was more like having a chronic illness for the rest of your life.

"I'm sure he wasn't interested in me that way," Vanessa protested. "If he was, he didn't pursue anything." Then she added, "At the time I was drawn to him, not romantically, but in a maternal way. In a weird way, he reminded me of Aiden—young and a bit immature, yet trying to make something of himself. Silly now that I look back at it. Boyd wasn't interested in anything but placing blame for everything that happened to him on someone else. Nothing was ever his fault, oh, no. It was everyone else out to get him."

"Then why target you as someone who wronged him?"

"I have no idea." She was silent for another block, then added, "And just so you know, I was working the night shift the night the dogs were let loose from their kennels. I know everyone believes Boyd had help from inside the base, but it wasn't me. I'm not the one helping him."

Isaac was surprised by the sudden vehemence in her tone. "I didn't suggest you were."

"Well, that's something, I guess," she said, her tone faintly bitter. "There are others, including the anonymous blogger, who have made it clear they believe I sent the rose to myself to deflect suspicion. The latest theory is that Boyd is getting help from a woman on base."

He hadn't realized the depth of what she'd been going through over the past few months. "That's a tough break, but I'm a witness to the attack who will exonerate you once and for all."

She lightly rubbed her neck, wincing at the tenderness. "Pictures of the bruises likely to be visible by morning should help, right?"

The thought of her golden skin marred by bruises infuriated him. If he'd been a minute later… He clenched his jaw, unwilling to think about how he may have stumbled across Vanessa's dead body.

The level of hatred Boyd was carrying around with him was inconceivable. Must be that Boyd wanted more from Vanessa, a personal relationship of some kind. No other explanation made sense. She must have done something, or said something, that dented his fragile ego.

No point rehashing it now. She needed protection, and he intended to make sure Captain Blackwood provided it to her. Isaac wasn't going to leave her alone, not until a Security Forces cop was stationed outside her house.

They walked the next block in silence.

At the corner, Vanessa took a left, heading past a thick hedge separating two front yards. A movement in the shrubbery caught his eye at the same time that Tango made a whining sound in the back of his throat.

Not a growl, but still a sound of distress.

Vanessa stopped dead in her tracks, reaching out to tightly grab his arm. "Did you hear that?" she whispered.

"Yes." Isaac's pulse kicked up and he instinctively pushed Vanessa behind him in an effort to protect her. "Call the police."

The movement in the bushes increased and Tango strained on his leash as if desperate to rush over.

Was Boyd hiding in there? Did he right now have a gun trained on them?

For a split second, his mind went back to the moment his chopper had been hit by enemy fire, spinning helplessly out of control. Temporarily lost in the past, he let go of Tango's leash and the dog took off straight toward the bushes.

No! Stay focused on the here and now!

"Tango!" His voice came out in a strangled cry, but the golden retriever didn't listen. The dog disappeared into the bushes.

Leaving Isaac as the only protector for Vanessa.

TWO

Vanessa wasted several precious minutes fumbling in her bag for her phone. When she finally found it, she punched in the emergency number for the base police. "This is Lieutenant Gomez and I'm with Captain Isaac Goddard. We're on the corner of Webster and Viking and have reason to believe Boyd Sullivan is hiding in the bushes. Hurry!"

"I'll send someone over," the Security Forces dispatcher promised.

She kept the phone in one hand and gripped the back of Isaac's uniform with the other. Her entire body began to shake, and she abruptly understood a small part of what Aiden and Isaac went through while battling their illness.

The thought of coming face-to-face with Boyd Sullivan made her break out in a cold sweat. She'd never felt helpless and vulnerable like this, until tonight. First the attack, and now this.

"The cops from the south gate are closest," she said in a low voice. "I'm sure they'll be here soon."

"I know." Isaac's hands were fisted, his elbows flexed at his side, as if he were expecting a physical fight.

Tango emerged from the bushes, tail wagging. He stood looking at them for a moment, then turned to duck back between the branches.

She frowned. "What was that about?"

"I'm not sure. Tango is a therapy dog, but he's still trained well enough to know when danger is near."

"So, Boyd isn't hiding in there?"

"Probably not. Stay here. I'll be right back." Isaac took a step forward, but she didn't let go of his uniform, choosing to go with him rather than remain on the street alone.

"Vanessa, you should stay here." Frustration was audible in his tone.

She shook her head. "Better to stick together."

Tango came out of the bushes again, gave a sharp bark and wheeled around to return to the brush. She relaxed her grip on Isaac's uniform, sensing the dog wanted them to follow.

Surely, the golden wouldn't lead them into harm's way.

"Call off the cops," Isaac said, parting the branches with one hand and using his flashlight app on his phone to illuminate the darkness. "False alarm."

She inwardly debated letting the police come anyway, since she needed to report her attack, but she would rather talk to Justin personally. Decision made, she called the dispatcher back, confirming there was no immediate danger and that the call could be canceled. She slipped the phone back into her bag, then crept closer, hearing the rustling and odd whimpering sounds before her eyes landed on a cluster of puppies.

"Did we find some of the lost dogs?" Six months ago, Boyd Sullivan or his accomplice had sneaked onto base and let nearly every single K-9 in the Working Dog Program out of their kennels, a little over two hundred of them. Over time many of the lost animals had been found, but there were still several missing, including three extremely valuable German shepherds named Glory, Scout and Liberty.

"I'm not sure. There are four pups here, but it's odd because there's no sign of the mother. I doubt the mother is one of the lost dogs or we would have found her by now. The puppies appear healthy and well cared for, so I don't think she abandoned them without a good reason."

"She must be one of the training dogs, don't you think? Maybe she was attacked by a coyote?" It was horrible to think of a pack of coyotes ganging up on the mom, who likely would have attempted to lure the predator away from her babies. "We have to try to find her."

"Agreed, although we need to get these pups to safety first." He gestured to the puppies. "These look to be a few weeks old—not that I'm an expert. And they're snuggled together to stay warm."

"My house is at the end of this block. Let's bring the puppies there and get them warmed up, then let the cops know what happened." Vanessa wondered how Aiden would like the puppies. Her brother tolerated Eagle, her Doberman, but didn't find any comfort in the animal. And while she was hopeful he'd connect with a therapy dog such as Tango, he'd already failed in the first attempt to match him up. Ruby, the first dog who'd been assigned to him, had been a loving Irish setter, but Aiden hadn't connected with Ruby on any level. Perhaps the adorable puppies might have a better chance of getting through to him.

Not that there was any guarantee that Master Sergeant Westley James, the lead trainer at the K-9 training center, would allow her and Aiden to care for them. Although if the mother wasn't one of the missing dogs, maybe he wouldn't mind?

She sent up a quick prayer, asking for God's

grace and mercy in keeping the puppies and the lost mother safe.

"You take two, and I'll take two," Isaac said, gathering a couple of the puppies in his broad hands and handing them over. She cradled them against her chest, marveling at the softness of their fur and their adorable faces.

"When we get the puppies settled and you're safe, I'll come back and search for the mother," Isaac said. "I'll also check with the veterinary clinic. They might have an injured dog that may belong to these pups."

"All right." As her small ranch home came into view, Vanessa picked up the pace, suddenly desperate to see her brother. She'd been gone far longer than her normal twelve-hour shift, and Aiden didn't always handle being on his own very well.

The house was mostly dark except for a lone light in the corner of the living room. Awash with guilt, she shifted the puppies to one arm, and fished for her keys to unlock the door. Using her hip, she pushed the front door open and stepped inside.

"Aiden? It's me, Vanessa. I'm home."

Isaac followed her inside, but remained near the doorway, instinctively giving her brother time to adjust to the presence of a stranger.

"Aiden?" She swept her gaze over the living

room, then noticed her brother sitting on the floor in a corner of the room, his face buried in his hands. "I'm sorry I'm late," she said in a low voice. "But look what I found. Puppies!"

Aiden lifted his head, his gaze darting anxiously around the room, and instantly zeroing in on Isaac and Tango standing near the door. "Who is he?" Aiden asked harshly, his expression contorted in a mask of anger. "Why is he here?"

Her heart sank as she realized how Aiden had struggled in her absence. Eagle came out of the kitchen to greet her, but with her hands full, she couldn't give her canine protector the attention he deserved.

She stayed focused on Aiden. "This is Captain Isaac Goddard, and he helped me bring the puppies home. Maybe you could hold them while I find a box to put them in?"

Aiden's gaze remained fixed on Isaac for a long moment before he finally noticed the squirming animals in her arms. Her brother's expression softened and he rose to his feet.

"Where did you find them?" he asked in a hushed tone.

"In the bushes near Webster and Viking," Isaac said from the doorway. "Four pups. I'm sad to say their mother seems to be missing. We're hoping she's getting care at the vet."

She wished Isaac would have remained silent, concerned that Aiden would become upset again from simply hearing his deep voice, but she needn't have worried. Aiden's gaze locked on the puppies and he came over to take one of them from her hands, bringing him up to his cheek.

"They're so soft," Aiden whispered. He met her gaze. "There's really four of them?"

"Yes." She handed him the second pup and then stepped back, subtly swiping at her damp eyes. The way her brother responded so positively to the puppies was more than she could have hoped for. "I'll find a box."

"There's one full of old movies next to my bed," Aiden said. "Just dump them on the floor."

She took a moment to give Eagle a welcoming rub between the ears before hurrying into Aiden's bedroom to empty the box of movies. When she returned, she was shocked to see that Isaac had come farther into the room and was standing less than three feet from Aiden.

What was he thinking? Shouldn't he have stayed near the door? What if Aiden freaked out again?

"Found it," she said as she rejoined them. Isaac set his two puppies in the box first, then her brother did the same. When she realized she'd been holding her breath, she let it out in a soundless sigh.

Tango and Eagle sniffed at each other curiously, but both dogs were trained well enough not to growl. Tango in particular was a calm, sensitive dog, the kind she'd hoped to get for Aiden one day.

"The pups might be hungry." Aiden's expression was full of concern.

"You're right," Isaac said in a low, nonthreatening tone. "They'll need warm milk for starters, but I'm not sure if cow milk is good for them. Vanessa, why don't you call the training center to see what you'll need to do in order to care for the puppies?"

"Good idea." She picked up her bag and dug out her phone. The call to the training center was immediately picked up by Master Sergeant Westley James, the training center operations director.

"This is Lieutenant Vanessa Gomez. Captain Isaac Goddard and I found four puppies, without any sign of the mother. We're not sure what breed they are, maybe a cross between a Lab and a rottweiler. We'd like to foster them, if you'll allow it."

"Found them where?"

"Less than a block from my house on Webster." She glanced at Isaac, then added, "Captain Goddard is going to head out to find the mother, see if she's somewhere close by. In the meantime, would you like us to bring the puppies into the vet?"

"That would be good. I'll meet you there."

"Okay, but if you don't mind, Aiden would really like to help foster the puppies." She knew Westley was aware of Aiden's need for a therapy dog and how miserably her brother had failed with Ruby. "It would be a great experience for us. Please? Just tell us what you'd like us to do."

There was a pause then a sigh. "Okay, you and Aiden can foster them for now. But I'm warning you, it's a time-consuming process. Any idea how old the puppies are?"

"We're not sure," she admitted. "But they're bigger than newborns. Maybe a few weeks?"

"I hope you're right, because we have a better chance of success if they're at least three to four weeks old. Once we determine how old they are, you can get the appropriate commercially prepared puppy formula and instructions on how to start solid foods, along with how to housebreak them."

"We can do that. Thank you." The wave of relief was overwhelming. She disconnected the call and smiled at Aiden. "Westley gave us permission to foster, but warned me it's a lot of work."

"I don't mind." Aiden held the cardboard box

in his arms as if he wasn't ever going to let it go, the expression on his face full of wonder and joy.

"Great. Then we've been ordered to bring them to the vet, and they'll provide everything we need."

"Okay." To her surprise, Aiden looked at Isaac. "We should probably take my sister's car, right?"

"Good idea."

Vanessa blinked the sting of tears away at Aiden's tentative acceptance of Isaac. Already they were bonded by the puppies and with that as a foundation, it was possible that Isaac's willingness to talk to Aiden would also help him learn better coping strategies.

Being attacked by Boyd Sullivan may have been the worst part of her day, but finding the puppies turned out to be the absolute best thing to have happened.

There was no doubt in her mind that these four tiny balls of fur were exactly what Aiden needed to help battle his illness.

And she'd do anything in her power to see her tormented brother relax and smile again.

Anything.

Isaac easily saw himself in Aiden's demeanor, from the tense anxiety emanating from the young man's very being, to the fear and anger darkening his brown eyes, replicas of his older sister's.

The kid was young, barely twenty from his estimation, and suddenly Isaac wished that the minimum age to enter the military was older than a mere eighteen.

Not that he wasn't proud to serve his country, because he was. After all, he'd gone straight into the Air Force Academy in Colorado, and from there to flight school to become an Air Force combat pilot. By the time he'd served his first tour overseas, he'd been twenty-three.

Now that he was thirty, his first tour seemed a lifetime ago.

There was no way to prepare for being deployed, although the various branches of the military did their best. Logically, he knew it wasn't as if every airman, soldier, marine or seaman experienced combat, but still, the exposure to violence certainly took its toll.

Which was why he still hadn't signed the paperwork to reenlist. Returning to the air as a pilot wasn't an option now. He'd never risk other lives by flying with PTSD. Which left a huge question mark on his future.

But that was not a problem to solve tonight.

As they stepped outside to Vanessa's car, he did a quick sweep of the neighborhood, looking for any sign of the puppies' mother. Tango helped, but he came up empty-handed.

He climbed into the car beside Vanessa, and she drove directly to the veterinary clinic. The vet, Captain Kyle Roark, greeted them when they arrived.

"Westley called me about the puppies. I think I may have the injured mother inside. Someone turned her in a few hours ago. She suffered a rather serious animal bite that required surgery to repair. I think she'll be fine, but I'll need to watch her closely for the next few days for signs of infection."

"Is she one of the training dogs?" Isaac asked.

Kyle shook his head. "No microchip. But I'm concerned there may be a link between this dog and the person who let the others go."

Isaac didn't like the sound of that.

Kyle took the puppies into an examination room to assess their condition. He returned a short while later with good news.

"They're all surprisingly healthy, and they look to be about four weeks old." He glanced at Vanessa and Aiden as he continued, "I'll give you some supplies you'll need to foster them, okay?"

"That would be great," Vanessa agreed.

Isaac had noticed how protective Aiden was of the puppies, and hoped Vanessa was making the right decision allowing him to help foster them. Not that he thought Aiden would hurt them in any way, but Isaac knew how horrible it was to be separated from an animal you'd bonded with.

He missed Beacon with an all-consuming intensity. For several days, after Beacon had saved his life in Afghanistan by dragging him by the back of his flight suit away from the burning chopper, he and the dog had hidden together in enemy territory while waiting to be rescued. Losing his best friend and Beacon's handler, Jake Burke, had been horrible. During those endless hours after the crash, Beacon had been his only source of comfort. Although even Beacon's reassuring presence couldn't keep his guilt at bay.

Then the USAF search-and-rescue chopper had arrived. The pilot had done a routine flyby, then circled around to land on a small level spot close to where he and Beacon had holed up. Getting into the chopper hadn't been easy, but by the time the rebels had begun firing at them, the pilot had gotten them airborne.

At first, he'd been overjoyed at being rescued, but when they'd landed in Kabul and he was separated from Beacon, his whole world had come crumbling down.

Not only had he failed Jake by crashing the chopper that caused his buddy's death, but he'd failed in keeping Jake's K-9 as he'd promised when they'd first begun flying together. Six months of red tape and politics and he still didn't have Beacon home.

But tomorrow was the day. Less than twenty-four hours and he'd have Beacon home where he belonged.

I'm trying, Jake. Just like I promised. I'll bring Beacon home!

Before the crash that had taken his buddy's life, he might have reached out to God for solace. But not anymore. These days, he didn't feel much like talking to God.

"We're ready to go," Vanessa said, pulling him from his troubling thoughts. "Isaac? Is everything okay?"

He nodded and cleared his throat. "Yep. All set."

Aiden had obviously delegated himself the primary caregiver as he picked up the box of puppies again and waited for Vanessa to get the door.

Vanessa's SUV had plenty of room for the three of them and the two dogs Eagle and Tango, not to mention the box of squirming puppies. Aiden kept the box on his lap the entire time, unwilling to let the puppies out of his sight.

Interesting how the Doberman stayed close to Vanessa's side, obviously trained to protect her.

If that was the case, why hadn't she brought the dog to the hospital with her? Granted, an intensive care unit probably wasn't an appropriate place for a dog, but surely under the circumstances an exception could be made for Vanessa's safety.

Aiden took the puppies inside and began feeding them, using the commercial formula provided by Kyle. He'd barely gotten settled when there was a sharp knock at the door. Vanessa answered it, looking surprised to see the head of the Security Forces standing there, his tall male Malinois named Quinn at his side.

"Why didn't you answer your phone?" Captain Justin Blackwood asked as he shouldered his way inside. Quinn stayed close, well trained enough not to react to the other dogs.

"Oh, I left my bag in the car while we were at the vet's office," she said with a guilty wince. "Sorry about that."

Justin scowled, glancing between Isaac and Vanessa. "Tell me what happened at the hospital."

Vanessa glanced over her shoulder, then gestured for the men to come into the living room. "I don't want my brother to hear this."

"Fine, but I need details," Justin insisted.

Isaac crossed his arms over his chest as Vanessa explained how she took a shortcut out of the hospital, going through the hallway containing offices to get to the other side of the building closest to the front entrance when the lights went out and strong hands grasped her around the neck.

Hearing her talk about the attack she'd suffered made Isaac angry all over again. Justin's expression turned grim as he inspected the red marks around her throat, already beginning to bruise.

"Did he say anything?" Justin asked.

Vanessa nodded. "I asked why and he said, 'Because you're in my way.'"

"In the way?" Isaac repeated. "Doesn't make sense. In the way of what?"

She shrugged her shoulder. "I don't know. In the way of his mission to eliminate the people who wronged him?"

"Then what happened?" Justin asked, looking at Isaac.

He and Justin knew each other from when they'd attended the Air Force Academy, but at the moment, he understood his friend was in charge of the ongoing investigation.

"I heard what sounded like a scuffle in the darkness and called out to see what was going on," Isaac said, relating his side of the story. "I found the light switch and turned it on in time to see Vanessa fall to the floor and a guy wearing black disappear down the stairwell. I made sure she was all right and left Tango with her, before going after him. Unfortunately, he was long gone."

"No description?" Justin asked, his blue eyes intense.

"Medium height and build. He wore a ski mask that covered his head so I can't tell you his hair color." Isaac shrugged. "I wish I could be more help."

Justin raked his hand across his short blond hair and let out a heavy sigh. "No proof that Sullivan is the assailant."

Vanessa bristled. "Boyd sent me a red rose. Who else has a grudge against me?"

Justin lifted a brow. "You were the one who said that you helped Boyd by providing first aid to him. Why would he have a score to settle with you?"

Vanessa's dark eyes flashed with anger. "I don't know, but I didn't attack myself, Captain."

"Come on, Justin, you know she didn't," Isaac added. "I saw him. And if I hadn't shown up, she'd be dead."

Justin let out a heavy sigh. "You're right. The marks on her neck are for real, so that means somewhere deep in Boyd's twisted mind, he's decided to come after her."

"And nearly killed her," Isaac added.

"I know, I know." Justin sounded tense.

Isaac arched an eyebrow at his friend. "Can you offer her round-the-clock protection?"

"I can have someone stationed outside the house at night, but we're short staffed so I don't have someone available to follow her around all day."

"I can protect her during the day." The offer popped out of his mouth before he had a chance to consider the consequences.

"I'm not sure that's necessary," Vanessa protested.

"I'll take whatever help you can give us," Justin said, ignoring her protest. "I'll keep someone stationed outside the house from nineteen hundred hours until zero seven hundred." He turned toward Vanessa. "You're probably safe enough here at home with Eagle during the day, but don't go anywhere alone, and keep Eagle close, too. Dobermans are instinctively protective."

"Nessa?" Aiden's voice from the doorway drew their attention. The young man cradled a puppy in his arms and stared at his sister with fear in his eyes. "What's going on?"

"Nothing to worry about, Aiden." Vanessa

crossed over to give her brother a hug. "Just extra protection for a while, no big deal."

Aiden didn't look as if he believed her, and Isaac didn't blame the kid. Vanessa was a lousy liar.

It was clear that Vanessa's life being in jeopardy impacted her brother in a big way. Isaac suspected if anything happened to her, Aiden wouldn't be able to handle it.

And even though he'd only just met Vanessa tonight, Isaac wasn't sure he'd be able to handle it, either.

THREE

"How are the puppies doing?" Vanessa crossed the living room to stand next to her brother. "We have to think of names for them."

Thankfully, Aiden's attention was diverted by the active pup in his arms as she'd hoped. "I was thinking about naming them after national parks. The two females could be Denali and Shenandoah, the males Smoky and Bryce."

"Those are awesome names." Vanessa stroked the puppy he held, wondering how they'd be able to tell them apart.

"You're in danger from Boyd Sullivan, aren't you?" Aiden asked abruptly.

She looked into her brother's mature-for-his-years gaze and knew she couldn't lie. "Yes. I'm afraid so. But Captain Blackwood is going to keep a cop stationed here at the house at night, so there's really nothing to worry about."

"You need to keep Eagle close from now

on," he said, his tone full of reproach. "Even at the hospital."

"I will." She forced a smile, knowing that Eagle wouldn't be allowed in an intensive care unit. "Do you need help feeding the rest of the litter?"

Aiden shook his head. "No, thanks." He looked at Isaac and Justin for a moment. "Make sure she's safe," he said, before disappearing into the kitchen.

"He'll be okay," Isaac said, reassuringly. "Just because he's struggling with an illness doesn't make him helpless."

"I know, but at twenty he's already been through so much…" Her voice trailed off as she glanced back at Aiden before joining the two men and the K-9 beside Justin. "Anything else you need from me?"

"Tell me more about this injured female dog that's at the veterinary clinic," Justin said with a frown. "It might be connected to our investigation."

"Captain Roark said she isn't from the training center," Isaac said. "The mother is a chocolate Lab, and the puppies appear to be a mix. Although he did mention there may be a link between this dog and the missing four from the training center."

"I have to agree," Justin said thoughtfully. "In

speaking with Gretchen Hill, the newest trainer on Westley's staff, she thinks it's possible the Olio Crime Organization may be involved with the dognapping. Three dogs are still missing, but when Patriot was returned, her collar had the letters *POCO* engraved on it. It's probably not a coincidence that the last three letters stand for Olio Crime Organization. Maybe even Property of Olio Crime Organization. I wonder if the injured chocolate Lab belonged to them at some point."

Vanessa's stomach clenched. "We assumed she was attacked by an animal, like a coyote, and Captain Roark agreed based on her wounds. Besides, how would someone from the Olio Crime Organization get on base? Fake ID? Or help from someone inside?"

"Anything is possible," Justin admitted. "A stretch, but possible. After all, it's looking more and more like the missing dogs were taken off base." He shrugged. "Right now, I can't see how the injured Lab would be linked, but I need to keep an open mind. There could be a connection."

She shivered at the horrible thought. "I'm sure it's a coincidence. We know coyotes have gotten on base, so it's likely she was injured protecting her pups. I doubt her presence on base is the result of foul play."

"Yeah, you could be right." Justin's tone lacked conviction.

There was a moment of silence before Isaac glanced at his watch. "It's late, we should go."

Justin nodded. "Don't forget, Vanessa, you'll have a cop stationed outside your house at night, and don't go anywhere alone. I placed a call while you were speaking with Aiden, and someone should be arriving any minute now."

"Understood." She walked the two men and their respective K-9s to the front door, Eagle staying close at her side. "Thanks," she said, glancing at Isaac. "For everything you did for me tonight. If there's ever anything I can do for you, just let me know."

A hint of a smile played at the corner of Isaac's mouth. "You're welcome." He paused, then added, "If you're not working tomorrow, maybe you'd be willing to go with me to meet Beacon's flight. It's due to arrive at fourteen hundred hours."

"I'm off tomorrow and would love to go. The idea of sitting around my house all day isn't at all appealing." She was touched that he'd asked, although she told herself not to read more into the offer than what it was at face value. A friend inviting a friend along to meet a plane, nothing more.

"Great, I'll stop by to pick you up." Isaac

smiled again, then turned and followed Justin out to the street, jumping into Justin's jeep beside him.

She stood in the doorway for a long moment, her hand resting on Eagle's silky head, watching as the red taillights of the jeep vanished into the darkness. She gave Eagle a few minutes out in the yard to do his business, then called him back inside.

A tall man with a Security Forces badge on his chest and navy blue beret on his head stepped up beside the doorway, offering a quick salute. "Everything okay, ma'am?"

"Of course. Good night." She returned the salute and ducked back inside. When Eagle joined her, she closed and locked the door behind her.

Aiden was still in the kitchen with the puppies, calling them by name as he worked on potty training. He took them out of the box and placed them on a spread of newspaper, praising them as they did their business.

"Good boy, Bryce. Denali, you're doing great, too. Shenandoah, stay on the paper, please. Smoky, you're a rock star. Nice job."

Watching her brother interacting positively with the pups filled her with hope and encouragement for his future.

Thank You, Lord, for answering my prayers!

"Are you going to keep them in the kitchen

for the rest of the night?" she asked, when all four pups had been cared for and the newspaper mess cleaned up.

"I'll stretch out on the sofa for a while, keep the box nearby." Aiden didn't meet her gaze and she knew that he often slept in the living room with the light on in an effort to minimize the nightmares.

"Let me know if you need help," she said. "Otherwise I'll see you in the morning."

Aiden nodded. She turned toward her bedroom when he called out, "Nessa?"

She looked over her shoulder. "What?"

"That guy, Isaac, is he going to be hanging around often?"

She hesitated, unsure how to respond. "We're just acquaintances, that's all. I only just met him today. Isaac has been suffering from nightmares and flashbacks, too, Aiden, just like you. We're not going to get involved, if that's what you're asking. Tomorrow the dog who saved his life will be returning to base, so I'm going along to support him while he picks Beacon up. I hope you don't mind, especially since Isaac seems determined to protect me."

Aiden shrugged. "I'm glad you won't be alone, but I don't want him to hurt you, the way that Leo guy did."

She was surprised to realize Aiden had heard

about her brief, misguided relationship with Leo Turner, an Air Force captain and one of the physicians she worked with at the hospital. She must have mentioned him during their FaceTime sessions while Aiden was overseas.

It bothered her that now that Aiden was back on base, he'd probably heard the rumors about Leo's multiple affairs. Her brother had enough to worry about without adding her welfare to the mix.

"Isaac and I are barely friends," she repeated firmly, for her brother's sake and her own. "He just wants to help keep me safe, that's all."

Bad enough she'd become the laughingstock of the ICU because she'd been oblivious to Leo's antics, until she'd seen the evidence for herself.

She didn't know if Isaac was the kind of guy to cheat on his girlfriend. What did it matter? She wasn't interested in a relationship. And Isaac had enough going on in his life, between Beacon's delayed homecoming and getting better.

Anything more than friendship would only get in the way.

Isaac had thought for sure he'd have trouble sleeping, considering the way he'd witnessed the attack on Vanessa, but surprisingly, he slept the entire night through.

He scrubbed a hand over his sandpaper-rough

jaw and marveled at how many times he'd slept through the night without being awoken from a nightmare. Months ago, they plagued him nightly. Now he only had them once a week, maybe less.

Logically, he knew that his issues weren't just because of Jake's death and the horrible experience of being shot out of the sky, but a culmination of several treacherous flights over enemy territory, always under fire, yet somehow managing to escape.

Until that last flight had killed Jake and his copilot, Kevin, leaving only him and Beacon.

He took several deep calming breaths to keep the memories at bay. Maybe he'd slept well because today was the day Beacon was coming home. The thought made him smile and he bolted out of bed to let Tango outside, then to shower, shave and dress.

As always, he took care of Tango first, providing the dog food and water, before grabbing a quick bite to eat. As he nursed a cup of coffee, his gaze fell on the reenlistment paperwork sitting in the center of the kitchen table. He pulled it toward him.

For several long seconds, he stared at the spot where he was supposed to sign his name. He'd have to pass a medical and psychological exam no matter what job he decided to do if he stayed in the Air Force, so why bother filling the stupid thing out? Maybe this was his time to get out of the military.

And do what?

He had no idea.

With a rough gesture, he shoved the paperwork aside. He still had several weeks yet before it was due. No point in dwelling on it now.

Today he only had one priority. Beacon.

After finishing his coffee, Isaac stared at Tango for a moment, then decided to take the dog for a walk. It was going to be a long day if he didn't find some way to occupy his time until Beacon's arrival.

Instantly, his thoughts went to Vanessa, Aiden and the four fostered puppies Aiden had named after national parks.

Nope. He shook his head. Not a smart idea to get too emotionally involved. Although, he had offered to talk to Aiden, hadn't he? And to keep Vanessa safe during the daytime hours?

Yes, he had.

She'd be safe with Eagle until he got there, so he took a quick walk around base to clear his head. He was secretly glad her house wasn't far from his as it would be easier to keep an eye on her.

He was thrilled when he'd found his place,

located on a dead-end street not far from the veterinary clinic.

Dogs were known to suffer from PTSD, too, and he used the fact to argue why he was the best fit for Beacon. With Jake gone, he was Beacon's best chance. He'd even gotten Jake's younger sister, Jacey, who was also a dog handler currently deployed overseas, to add her support.

He and the dog were two wounded warriors who deserved to be together. And the powers that be within the Air Force had finally agreed with him.

He ran into Captain Kyle Roark outside the veterinary clinic and waved him down. "Hey, any news on the female dog you operated on last night?"

Kyle nodded. "So far, she's holding her own. I have her on heavy-duty antibiotics and I'm keeping her sedated because of the extensive sutures. In my professional opinion she was likely attacked by a coyote."

"I'm happy to hear she's recovering. And an animal bite is better than the idea of humans hurting her on purpose," Isaac said with a heavy sigh. "At least now there's no reason to believe there's a possible connection to the Olio Crime Organization."

Kyle grimaced. "I'm not sure they're entirely out of the picture. No one living on base has reported a lost dog, aside from the training dogs that are still missing. A person within the crime ring may have sneaked the dog on base because she was pregnant and they wanted nothing to do with a litter of pups."

"Why?" Isaac asked. "They could dump her anywhere."

"Who knows how these guys think?" Kyle shook his head. "It's just odd that she showed up here, that's all. Anyone on base would take better care of their pet."

"Maybe." Done with the discussion of the injured dog, he turned his attention to the topic that had him anxious. "Are you going to be around later when Beacon arrives?"

Kyle's face lit up with a wide smile. "Wouldn't miss it."

"Great. I'll see you then." Isaac waved and took Tango home.

He did some chores around the house for a couple of hours. By lunchtime, he decided he couldn't stay home alone any longer. He picked up three meals to go from Carmen's, his favorite Italian restaurant, and brought them over to Vanessa's house.

He walked up to Vanessa's front door and rapped lightly.

A series of high-pitched yips could be heard

from inside, making him smile. Vanessa opened the door looking surprised to see him.

"Isaac, I wasn't expecting you for a couple of hours yet."

"I brought lunch from Carmen's," he said, lifting the bag as proof. "Enough pasta for all three of us."

Her expression softened as she realized he'd included Aiden. "Come in. Lunch will be a welcome break from the nonstop potty training going on around here."

"I can only imagine," he said with a chuckle. Inside, he nodded to her brother.

"Hey," Aiden greeted him cautiously.

"How are our four national parks doing?" he joked.

"They're awesome." Aiden placed the puppies back in their box. "Something smells good."

"Carmen's is always amazing." He set the bag in the center of the kitchen table as Vanessa and Aiden washed up at the sink. Vanessa was more beautiful than he remembered, with her dark wavy hair hanging loose around her shoulders. She wore her dress blues and he appreciated her delicate features.

Whoa, wait a minute. What was wrong with him? He'd been around plenty of attractive women before. Even since his former fiancée, Amber. None had even remotely raised his interest.

Until now.

Vanessa pulled out plates and silverware while Aiden fetched three bottles of cold water from the fridge. He opened the bag and pulled out the aluminum to-go containers of pasta, each still warm from the oven.

Vanessa took her seat, bowed her head and began to pray. "Dear Lord, we thank You for this food we are about to eat and for the friendship You have blessed us with. Keep Beacon and the puppies safe in Your care, Amen."

Despite his reservations about God and faith, Isaac thought of Beacon and found himself responding with a heartfelt "Amen."

"Amen," Aiden added, glancing down at the box of pups near his feet.

The spaghetti and meatballs from Carmen's were delicious, and as they ate, they discussed the puppies at length. Isaac was impressed at the responsibility Aiden was taking in caring for them, especially the way he'd found a way to identify each one by sight corresponding them to their name. Denali had a notch in her right ear and Shenandoah was the runt of the litter. Bryce had a small tan spot on his belly while the fur on the tip of Smoky's tail was black.

Vanessa seemed more relaxed, too, despite the bruises that darkened her neck. He was relieved to hear she'd used ice to keep the swelling down.

The time flew by and he soon realized they had to leave to avoid being late. He asked Aiden if he wanted to come with them, but the young man insisted on staying home to watch over the pups.

"I'm going to try some mash while you're gone," Aiden said with a wry grin. "Better that Nessa isn't here to watch, since Kyle warned me about how messy they'll get."

"Maybe you should feed them in the bathtub," Vanessa suggested, her expression half-joking. "That way you can contain the mess and go right into giving them a bath."

Aiden laughed at her suggestion. Vanessa looked so surprised, Isaac wondered how long it had been since she'd heard the sound of her brother's laughter.

Fostering the puppies was obviously a great job for him.

"I'll leave Eagle here with Aiden," Vanessa said. "I'm sure Beacon doesn't need the added stress."

Isaac hesitated, then nodded. "It's probably best."

"We'll take my SUV," Vanessa said. "I'll drive."

"Okay." After loading Tango into the back, he slid into the passenger seat beside her, wishing he was armed. But only Security Forces cops were armed on base, and as a pilot he couldn't carry one without special permission. As she drove, he kept a sharp eye out for anything suspicious.

Canyon Air Force Base was huge, covering over 600 acres. Roughly seven thousand people were on base at any given time, mostly military and some civilian. The airport runway was located on the north side of the base, a distance from the housing section.

Isaac swiped his damp palms against his jeans, unaccountably nervous. This was the moment he'd been waiting for since he arrived stateside.

Vanessa glanced at him. "Looks as if there's already a big crowd of people gathered there along with the media. I hope I can find a place to park."

Normally he wasn't a fan of crowds, but knowing Beacon would be getting off the plane in less than thirty minutes made the discomfort worthwhile.

They found a parking spot in front of the command offices and walked from there. With Tango at his side, he kept close to Vanessa as they walked, again keeping a keen eye on their surroundings. No easy task since there were literally hundreds of airmen and officers around.

Once they were situated at the front of the

crowd, he shielded his eyes from the sun with his hands, scanning the sky for the plane. There! A surge of excitement hit hard, although he told himself not to get his hopes up too high.

It wasn't that long ago that he'd stood in this exact same spot waiting for another plane supposedly bringing Beacon home. Only it hadn't been Beacon on the plane, but some other K-9. He'd suffered a relapse that night, despairing over the possibility of never seeing Beacon again.

At least this time, Vanessa was with him. He glanced over at her, amazed at what a difference it made to have someone supporting him.

He enjoyed spending time with her. She was easy to be around. Not nearly as demanding as Amber had been, or maybe he was just in a better place now than he had been back then. Considering he'd only first met Vanessa less than twenty-four hours ago, it was crazy how much he'd come to depend on her.

Only as a friend, he reminded himself. Once he had Beacon home, he wouldn't need this weird connection he seemed to have with her.

As the sound of the plane engine grew louder, his heart beat faster with anticipation. The C-130 Hercules aircraft used for transporting troops emerged from the clouds, approaching the runway.

When the wheels hit the tarmac, he realized he was holding his breath and clutching Vanessa's hand tightly in his. He released her with an apologetic smile.

She rested her hand in a reassuring gesture on his arm. The C-130 coasted to a stop, then angled toward the hangar.

He couldn't stop himself from taking several steps forward, urging Vanessa along with him as they separated themselves from the crowd.

The cargo door in the rear of the plane opened and a short runway ramp was lowered to the ground. A man wearing his battle dress uniform emerged first, holding a leash, then he caught a glimpse of the familiar black-and-gold German shepherd.

Beacon!

He must have shouted the dog's name out loud because the crowd burst into spontaneous applause.

The dog stood still for a moment, nose quivering. The animal must have picked up his scent, because he abruptly wheeled toward him, ears perked forward as if in recognition.

"Come, Beacon," he said, taking a step forward to meet the dog who'd saved his life.

The loud crack of a gunshot rang out.

The entire area erupted into panicked chaos. The airman holding Beacon's leash yanked the dog hard, diving for shelter as people began running and screaming, dropping to the ground and desperately seeking cover.

Vanessa pulled him down beside her. "Are you all right?" she asked breathlessly.

"I think so." He was numb from shock, but checked himself for signs of injury. No blood? Good sign. Thankfully, he didn't see any injuries on Vanessa or Tango, either. "I have to get to Beacon."

He tried to pull away from her, but she hung on with steely determination. "No, you might put the dog in danger."

The possibility made him sick to his stomach. Was Boyd really out there shooting at them? Why would Beacon have been the target? It didn't make any sense for Boyd to come after the dog.

What in the world was going on?

FOUR

From her position low on the ground, Vanessa swept her gaze over the area, searching for any sign of injuries to the people near her. It wasn't easy, because most of them were running every which way, desperate to seek shelter from the gunman.

No evidence of bleeding wounds so far, but that fact was only slightly reassuring.

Boyd must have been the one who'd taken a shot at Isaac's dog. Who else would do something so crazy? But why? It didn't make any sense.

Unless Beacon hadn't been the true target. She shivered, despite the heat.

She remembered feeling something whizzing past her face. Was it possible the bullet was meant for her? She'd been standing in a direct line in front of Beacon.

"Beacon!" Isaac's voice was hoarse with fear. "I don't see him. Where did he go?"

She tightened her grip on Isaac's arm, determined to prevent him from running directly toward the plane. "The handler will keep him safe."

Isaac didn't look convinced. "I think Beacon may be hurt. It looked as if he may have hit the side of the C-130 when the handler jerked him out of the line of fire."

"We'll check it out." She kept her tone calm, worried Isaac might suffer a relapse between the sound of gunfire and the crazed chaos surrounding them. The crowd was thinning so they couldn't stay here. They needed to move. The runway was clear, but what if the gunman was still out there? Better to try losing themselves in the crowd.

"This way." Isaac rose to his feet, clutching Tango's leash.

She nodded. "I'm with you."

Isaac gently propelled her protectively in front of him, toward a large group of people exiting the area, as if he'd read her mind. "We'll circle around to the other side of the plane."

"Understood." She continued to watch the people around her for injuries. Security Forces cops swarmed the area in search of the gunman. She hoped and prayed they'd find Boyd, or whoever the shooter was.

"Help me! Someone please help me!"

Vanessa stopped and turned toward the sound of crying. A woman was crouched on the ground, clutching her ankle.

"Isaac, hold up." She detoured toward the sobbing woman, kneeling beside her. "What happened?"

"I was crushed in the crowd." The woman swiped at her face in an attempt to pull herself together. "I was pushed down and someone stomped on my ankle." She sniffed and swiped at her face again. "Do you think it's broken?"

The ankle was swollen and starting to bruise, so it was entirely possible. "You'll need to have that x-rayed."

Isaac dropped down beside them. "We better call an ambulance."

On cue, the wail of sirens rose above the din. "They're almost here." She glanced at Isaac. "I'll stay here with her, if you want to go ahead to find Beacon."

His gaze flickered with indecision, but then he shook his head. "I'm not leaving you alone. We'll make sure she's cared for first."

She flashed a grateful smile and then attempted to catch the attention of an ambulance that had just arrived. But she was just one person in a sea of people. Fortunately, one of the cops noticed her and ran over.

"Crowd crush injury," Vanessa told him. "I'm

a nurse from the hospital. Do you know if anyone else is hurt?"

"Only minor bumps and bruises so far from what I can see." The cop's expression was grim. "Could have been much worse."

"I know." Vanessa silently thanked God for watching over the men and women on base. "She needs a lift to the hospital for X-rays."

"Understood." The cop jogged toward the ambulance, waving his arm. Two paramedics jumped out, grabbed a gurney and headed in their direction.

Once the injured woman was safely on her way to the hospital, she turned back to Isaac. "Let's go find Beacon."

He nodded, placing his hand on the small of her back, keeping her ahead of him.

Hyperaware of the heat radiating from his fingers, she did her best to stay focused. As they approached the opposite side of the runway, two cops identified by their dark blue berets stepped in front of them, blocking their path. They both saluted, then stood at attention.

"We need to get through," Vanessa said, after returning their salute.

"This is a restricted area, ma'am," the taller of the two said. "You both need to clear out."

Isaac frowned. "I'm Captain Goddard, and

Beacon is my dog," Isaac said in an authoritative tone. "I need to make sure he's okay."

"I'm sorry, sir, but as I said, this is a restricted area," the taller cop repeated. "I'm afraid you'll need to make other arrangements."

She felt Isaac tense and tried to think of a way past these guys.

"Isaac?" A familiar voice caught her attention. She glanced over to see Captain Kyle Roark, waving at Isaac from behind the two cops. The vet sent him a reassuring smile. "Don't worry, I have it under control."

"Is Beacon all right?" Isaac asked. "He wasn't hit by gunfire, was he?"

"No, he wasn't shot. He'll be fine." A shadow crossed Kyle's eyes. "Try not to stress about this, Isaac. I'm taking Beacon to the clinic. You can visit him there later, okay?"

The hope in Isaac's eyes wilted away, replaced by panic. "The clinic? Why? What happened?"

Kyle made his way through the cops to face Isaac. "Beacon wasn't hit by a bullet or anything, but he does have a bad laceration and possible head injury."

Isaac went pale. Vanessa grasped his arm in an attempt to keep him grounded. "Did that happen when the handler jerked him out of the way?"

Kyle winced. "I'm afraid so. His head hit the

edge of the plane. But I think he's going to be fine. This is merely a precaution, okay? I just want to watch him for a couple of days."

"Yeah, I get it." Isaac's shoulders slumped in defeat.

Vanessa's heart went out to him. She knew how much Isaac had been looking forward to being reunited with Beacon. Especially after all this time. Six months was a long time and now this latest issue was yet one more obstacle thrown into his path.

The vet turned and made his way back through the restricted area to care for Beacon.

"Come on, Isaac." She forced a smile. "Let's get out of here. Beacon is in good hands with Kyle."

"I know." Isaac's voice was low and rough. "I hope he's right about the injury not being serious. If anything happens to Beacon…" His voice trailed off.

She squeezed his arm. "It won't." She edged away from the two cops, unwilling to talk in front of them. Isaac and Tango followed. "Let's try to look on the bright side. Beacon is here, on base. Home at last. He'll be staying with you 24/7 in no time."

Isaac nodded, but the light in his eyes had been replaced with a dull acceptance.

They walked to her SUV in silence. She

opened the doors and windows to let the hot air out, then cranked the air-conditioning.

"Do you want me to drop you off?" she asked, as Isaac stared blindly through the windshield.

"Huh?" He turned toward her. "No, I'm here to help keep you safe, remember? And after this latest issue, I think I need to stick close."

She nodded, put the SUV in gear and edged into traffic. There were still a lot of people trying to get away from the landing strip, so there was no point in hurrying.

Isaac seemed to be concentrating on the area around them as she drove, and she was touched by his determination to protect her. She couldn't remember the last time any man had cared enough to do something like this.

It took a full thirty minutes to go five miles, but from there traffic thinned so that it was easy enough to reach her house. She hoped Aiden hadn't heard about the gunshot. She didn't want him to worry or to have a flashback.

Her brother had come so far in one day of taking care of the puppies. She'd hate to see him suffer a relapse now.

When she pulled into her short driveway, though, she was surprised to find Captain Blackwood and his K-9, Quinn, standing outside her front door. When Justin caught sight of her, he and Quinn loped over to meet her.

"Did you see what happened?" he demanded.

She suppressed a sigh and glanced at Isaac. He shrugged and slid out from the vehicle, letting out Tango. She came around the front of the car to join the two men.

"No," she said, belatedly answering Justin's question. "I heard the shot, and then everything went crazy. I thought I felt something whizz past me, but honestly, I can't even tell you what side of the landing strip the shot came from."

"I didn't see much, either," Isaac added. "My gaze was focused on Beacon. The handler reacted instantly, jerking Beacon out of the way, but the dog suffered a head injury as a result."

"The shooter must have been Boyd." Justin let out a frustrated sigh. "And he must have help on base, or I'm sure we would have found him by now."

"I don't understand why he'd shoot at Beacon," Isaac said. "That's the part that doesn't fit with what I've heard about the Red Rose Killer."

Vanessa straightened her shoulders and lifted her chin. "I'm not sure Beacon was the target."

Justin pinned her with a glare. "Who was?"

"Me." She lifted her hands, palms facing upward. "Boyd attacked me last evening. Why not follow me out to the airstrip to try again?"

"I don't know about that." Justin frowned.

"I was directly in front of Beacon." Vanessa

touched the bruises on her neck. She felt certain, deep in her bones, that she was the intended target.

Only this time, she'd put Isaac, Beacon and hundreds of other innocent people in danger, too.

Isaac wanted to put a reassuring arm around Vanessa, but held back, loath to make her uncomfortable in front of Justin. Isaac cleared his throat. "Actually, it's possible I was the target."

Vanessa reared back, staring at him in surprise. "You? Why?"

He shrugged. "Why not? Beacon's homecoming has been in the news for months now. Everyone on base knew I'd be there today."

"Have you met Boyd? Talked to him? Interacted with him in any way?" Vanessa peppered him with questions. "Is there a reason for him to be upset with you?"

"No, I've never met him that I'm aware of," Isaac admitted. "I've studied his mug shot. His face doesn't ring any bells. But this guy seems to be offended at the smallest transgression. For all I know, he thinks I did something to him. Or maybe he doesn't like me stealing his limelight."

Justin crossed his arms over his chest with a scowl. "Boyd never made it out of basic training, so there's no reason for him to go after a combat pilot. Or your dog."

"What's your theory, then?" Isaac pressed.

Justin's lips thinned. "I don't have one yet. I prefer to deal with facts. Vanessa may have been the target, but at this point, all I know is that someone fired a shot in a crowd of people. I've heard from Security Forces that no deaths or gunshot wounds have been reported. That tells me the shooter isn't a Canyon sniper. Someone we trained wouldn't have missed."

Vanessa nodded slowly. "You're right. The shooter must be someone with less experience."

"Boyd fits the profile," Isaac said. "Considering he didn't finish basic."

Justin's smile was grim. "You're right, Boyd wasn't a good marksman. He could have been aiming for Vanessa and missed by a mile."

"Or he could have simply shot toward the dog out of spite," Vanessa offered. "Can't you see him sitting back and enjoying the sheer panic he'd caused?"

"I can." Isaac suspected Boyd had self-esteem issues; why else would he be lashing out at anyone who'd wronged him? He glanced at Blackwood. "You need to catch him, and soon."

"Tell me about it." Justin's tone was flat and hard. "He's making all of us look like idiots by being on the loose this long. Which is why I'm convinced someone is helping him." Justin shot an apologetic glance at Vanessa. "I'm sorry I ever suspected you. Since you helped him once before, I thought it was possible you did again."

Vanessa massaged the bruise around her neck. "I understand, but trust me. I wouldn't help him do something like this. I'm a nurse, so it's hard for me to ignore someone who is hurt." Her brown eyes were large and pleading. "That's the only reason I stopped to help Boyd all those years ago."

Isaac stepped closer to her in a show of support. "You're not a suspect anymore," he reassured her.

"No, you're not." Justin regarded her thoughtfully. "But it's clear you're next on Boyd's list. Be careful, understand? Keep Isaac and Eagle close."

"I will."

The front door opened and Vanessa's brother stood there, looking at the three of them uncertainly. "Something wrong?"

"Hi, Aiden. How are our national parks doing?" Vanessa dropped her hand from her throat and headed toward her brother.

"Great." There was a lack of enthusiasm in his tone.

Justin excused himself and headed to his vehicle with Quinn. Isaac moved toward Vanessa and Aiden, hoping she didn't close her brother out of the truth.

Suffering from PTSD was bad, but being lied to never helped. People thought softening the facts was the way to go, but he'd always hated it.

"Someone shot a gun into the crowd at the landing strip," Vanessa said. "But no one was seriously hurt. Beacon suffered a laceration and head injury, though."

Aiden's fingers closed into fists. "Boyd?"

"Possibly, but we don't know for sure." Isaac stepped forward. "I want you to know I'll be staying close in order to protect your sister."

Aiden's brown gaze, so much like Vanessa's, met his. "Thanks for telling me the truth."

"Always," Isaac said.

"I'm sorry about Beacon," Aiden added.

"Me, too. But he's in good hands with the vet." Isaac glanced anxiously at his watch. How much time did Kyle need to examine the dog? He needed to see Beacon up close with his own eyes, to know without a shadow of a doubt the dog would be okay.

"The puppies are doing okay?" Vanessa asked again.

This time, Aiden's smile was genuine. "They're great. They loved the mash I gave them. And I fed them in the bathtub, like you suggested.

Worked perfectly. And they enjoyed the bath that followed."

"I'm glad." Vanessa gave her brother a one-armed hug.

Isaac was thrilled to hear Aiden was bonding with the puppies. He knew from personal experience how helpful it was to have that connection.

Like the one he had with Beacon.

"I'd like to head over to the clinic," he told her. "But don't want to leave you unprotected."

"I'll go with you," Vanessa offered.

He hesitated. It seemed that ever since he'd rescued Vanessa from Boyd's attack, he'd been leaning on her for strength and support. That wasn't what he'd intended. She was the one who needed his protection.

And staying here at her house with Eagle at her side was probably the best way to keep her safe. Being with him at the airstrip hadn't worked out so well.

"It's okay," he said, averting his gaze. "I'm just going to pop in quick. I won't stay long."

"I'm coming with you," she said, as if she wasn't taking no for an answer. "You shouldn't be alone at a time like this."

He'd hated it when Amber had treated him like an invalid, but for some reason, he didn't have the same negative emotional response toward Vanessa. "Are you sure you won't feel safer here at home?"

"I'm sure. Justin said I could go out as long as I was with someone and had Eagle with me. I'd actually like to see how Beacon is for myself." Her brow puckered in a frown. "Especially since his injury is my fault."

"It's not," he protested. "If you want to blame someone, blame Boyd. He's the bad guy, not you."

Vanessa turned toward Aiden. "Are you okay here for a while longer?"

"Sure." Aiden glanced over his shoulder at what Isaac assumed was the box of puppies. "It's almost time for the next bout of potty training."

Vanessa laughed and Isaac found himself smiling in response to the joyous sound.

It had been a long time since he'd had something to be happy about.

"Come, Eagle," Vanessa called her K-9 protector out and came up beside Isaac. "This time, you're coming with us. Time to go."

"I'd rather walk, if you don't mind," Isaac said. He didn't trust himself behind the wheel since he'd been back on base. And especially now, after the recent gunfire.

Vanessa readily nodded in agreement, and the walk to the veterinary clinic didn't take long. Isaac held the door open for her, then glanced over his shoulder, feeling as if someone might be watching them.

But of course, there wasn't. He told himself he had a right to be paranoid, but he also knew it was a side effect of his PTSD. Most of the time he was able to keep it under control.

Today had been a challenge. When the shot was fired, for a moment he'd gone back to the cockpit of the chopper he was manning when it had been struck by enemy fire. And though he'd tried to focus on Beacon, the dog had vanished from sight.

With Vanessa's help, he'd managed to stay grounded in the here and now. But it hadn't been easy.

"Can I help you?" a perky receptionist greeted them warmly when they entered the clinic. She eyed their respective dogs. "Do your dogs need a checkup?"

"No," Isaac said. "I'm here to see Beacon."

The receptionist looked confused for a moment. "Oh, you mean the shepherd that was just brought in by Captain Roark?"

"Yes. Will you please let him know Captain Isaac Goddard is here?"

"Of course, please excuse me." She disappeared, and it was all Isaac could do not to follow her back to find Kyle and Beacon for himself.

Thankfully she returned a few minutes later.

"Captain Roark will meet you in exam room number three."

Finally! "Thank you."

He and Vanessa crowded into the small room with Eagle and Tango. He thought about Tango, wondering if Westley would reassign the therapy dog to someone else once Kyle discharged Beacon into his care. Tango was a great dog, and Isaac was sure that he'd be a wonderful companion to the next airman who needed him.

Two long minutes later, the door opened and Kyle came in carrying Beacon. The dog was large, so it was no easy task, but the vet gently placed Beacon on the exam table.

The laceration along the side of Beacon's head made the blood drain from Isaac's face. Vanessa grabbed his arm and moved closer.

"Hey, Beacon." Isaac eased forward and held out his hand for the animal to sniff. "Remember me?"

Beacon buried his nose in Isaac's hand, his tail thumping against the stainless-steel table. Isaac felt tears of relief burn his eyes, and he bent down to press his face against Beacon's fur.

"You're home now, boy," he murmured. "I'm not leaving you again."

"He's going to be fine, Isaac," Kyle said. "I did a CT scan of his brain and there's no sign of an intracranial bleed. Give me a day or two to watch over him, and Beacon here will be good to go."

Isaac nodded, knowing it was for the best that he stay at the clinic. The animal's health was all that mattered.

He felt Vanessa's hand on his back and between her comforting touch and Beacon being home, he knew he'd reached another milestone on his path to healing.

And for the first time in a long while, he silently lifted his heart and thanked God for everything he'd been given.

FIVE

The way Isaac hugged Beacon warmed Vanessa's heart. The bond between the dog and the fighter pilot was palpable. Clearly, after all this time, they deserved to be together.

Thinking of the reckless gunshot fired into the crowd at the landing strip earlier that afternoon made her temper simmer.

Boyd Sullivan needed to be found and arrested soon.

"Thanks, Kyle," Isaac murmured, stepping back from the exam table. "I appreciate getting a few minutes with Beacon, and everything you're doing for him."

"That's my job, remember?" Kyle pointed out with a smile. "But hey, I'm glad he's doing okay, too."

She dropped her hand from Isaac's back, suddenly feeling self-conscious about the warmth of his skin radiating through his shirt. "That makes three of us."

"Do you mind if I stop by again tomorrow morning?" Isaac asked.

Kyle hesitated, then nodded. "Sure, we open at zero nine hundred."

It was on the tip of Vanessa's tongue to offer to accompany Isaac again, but then remembered she was scheduled to work a twelve-hour shift. Besides, Isaac didn't need her assistance. Sure, he was supposed to protect her, but if she were honest with herself, she would admit she wanted to be with Isaac for purely selfish reasons.

Because she liked him. More than she should. They'd only just met, but she felt as if she'd known him for weeks rather than a couple of days.

They left the veterinary clinic, stepping back into the bright sunlight. Isaac paused to sweep his gaze over the area, taking his role as protector seriously. She looked at him curiously, and he shrugged, gesturing toward the Winged Java Café. "It seems safe enough. Would you like some coffee or sweet tea?"

His request caught her off guard, but her heart leaped with anticipation. "Sure."

They walked down the street with the dogs between them and claimed the first empty outside table shaded by a yellow umbrella. Isaac held out her chair for her, but remained standing. "What would you like?"

She normally didn't drink caffeine this late in the afternoon. "An iced coffee, but decaf, please."

"You got it." Isaac went inside to place their order. She felt funny sitting there waiting for him, as if this was some sort of date.

It wasn't. Isaac was just being courteous. The same way he'd been when he'd brought over lunch from Carmen's.

She went still. Was she wrong about what was happening here? Maybe Isaac was trying to be more than just friends with her.

The image of her ex-boyfriend Leo filled her mind. He'd seemed nice, and protective and wonderful, too, but it had all been an act.

Leo liked women. Many women. She had no clue why he'd bothered to ask her out.

She pushed the memories aside and mentally reaffirmed she wasn't in the market for a relationship. Isaac was a nice guy who had not only agreed to protect her, but to talk to her brother. That was all that mattered.

To keep herself busy, she pulled out her cell phone and scrolled through her email. A notification from the anonymous blogger popped up. Ever since the blogger had put the idea that Vanessa was helping Boyd out there for everyone to read, she'd made sure to follow the blog so she could keep track of the ridiculous allegations.

Filled with dread, she clicked on the link to read what the phantom person had written this time.

Boyd Sullivan is back on base and obviously dumber than a box of rocks for continuing to come back to Canyon. He should be on his way to Mexico by now. That he's not means he's just asking to be caught!

"Are you kidding me?" she whispered in horror.

"What?" Isaac set down her iced decaf and then dropped his lanky frame into the seat beside her.

She gestured to her phone. "Have you seen the anonymous blogger's latest post?"

"May I?" He held out his hand for her phone. His emerald gaze grew tense and serious as he read the note. "Talk about waving a red flag at a bull."

"Right?" She sipped her iced coffee and shook her head. "Why would anyone rile Boyd up like this? The man is already unstable. Something like this could easily send him off the deep end."

Isaac returned her phone. "I agree. I'm surprised Justin hasn't shut down the site."

"Freedom of speech, right?" She couldn't hide the hint of bitterness in her tone. "If Boyd was the one who took the shot at Beacon, or at me, then we know he's armed. He could decide to go on a wild shooting rampage at any time." The very thought made her stomach churn with nausea. "Do you know how many people he could kill before one of ours manages to take him out? Too many."

"He's had plenty of time to stage a mass shooting if that was his goal," Isaac pointed out. "In my opinion, he's enjoying this cloak and dagger stuff far too much."

"You're probably right," she agreed, but she couldn't shake the sense of despair. Over the course of the last several years there had been too many mass shootings to count.

Some people would do anything for a moment of glory. Was Boyd Sullivan one of them?

She truly didn't know.

Isaac changed the subject to comment on Aiden's progress with fostering the pups. "He's really doing great with them, isn't he?"

She smiled. "Yes, I'm amazed at the difference in just twenty-four hours. As much as I feel bad for the pups' mother being attacked by a coyote, I'm thrilled Aiden has been given this opportunity."

"I'm happy to keep checking in on him, if you think it will help."

She was touched by his offer. "That would be

great. I know Aiden still has a ways to go, but every step forward gives me hope for his future."

Isaac nodded. "It's the same for me, too. Knowing Beacon is close is a start, but…" His voice trailed off, then he softly continued, "I'm still not sure how much I'll be able to manage my symptoms."

She understood that this was his way of warning her there couldn't be anything romantic between them. That he didn't consider her anything but a friend. And she felt foolish that she'd thought, even for a minute, otherwise.

"I know, Isaac." She lightly brushed her fingers over his tanned forearm. "It's okay." She drained her iced coffee. "Thanks again, but I should head home. I need to encourage Aiden to eat something for dinner, and I have to work early in the morning."

Isaac stood, his brow furrowed. "You're going to take Eagle with you to the hospital tomorrow, right?"

She glanced down at her faithful Doberman and reluctantly nodded. "Yes, I'll take him. But it's not going to be easy to look out for his needs while also caring for my patients. He can't be in the middle of the ICU with me and patient care has to come first."

"I don't want you to go to the hospital alone, so I'll walk you over early in the morning. That way, I can give you a hand with Eagle during your shift," Isaac offered.

"All right," she agreed, understanding he was just fulfilling his role as her protector.

He walked her home. Her phone rang as they reached the door. She pulled it out, frowning when she didn't recognize the number. It began with the base exchange, so she went ahead and answered it.

"Hello?"

"Next time, you won't get away," a gravelly voice said.

"Who is this?" she demanded, looking at Isaac. She could feel the blood draining from her face. Holding her breath, she waited for a reply.

But there was nothing but silence on the line.

"What did he say?" Isaac asked.

She drew in a shaky breath. "'Next time, you won't get away.'"

"I think I need to sleep on your sofa tonight," Isaac said, his expression troubled. "I don't like this at all."

"I don't, either." Her fingers trembled as she slipped the phone back in her pocket. Had the voice belonged to Boyd? She couldn't say one way or the other for sure. She swallowed hard and tried to pull herself together. "There will be a cop outside my door starting at nineteen hundred hours."

"Then I'll wait." Isaac put his hand in the center of her back and escorted her into the house.

She was grateful for his presence. They helped with the puppies until nineteen hundred hours.

"Are you sure you don't want me to stay?" Isaac asked.

"I'm sure." She forced a smile. "We'll be fine."

He hesitated, clearly not happy, but reluctantly nodded. "See you tomorrow, then."

"Okay." She watched him walk away and the minute he was out of sight, regretted her decision.

Later that night, as she slipped into bed, she relived the phone call over and over.

Then she bolted upright in bed as a horrible thought entered her mind. If the caller had been Boyd, how in the world had he gotten her personal cell number?

The next morning Isaac showed up as promised to escort her to the hospital. Vanessa reluctantly brought Eagle along, hoping it was the right decision to keep the animal inside for her twelve-hour shift. Dogs were not allowed in the intensive care unit, but her boss agreed that she could keep Eagle in the back nurses' workroom, away from the patients.

Still, it wasn't easy to concentrate when she was worried about how Eagle was doing.

Halfway through the day, Isaac arrived to take Eagle outside. She gratefully took him into the back room and handed him Eagle's leash. "Take him for a nice long walk, okay? I feel terrible that he's cooped up in here with me. It's not like Boyd is going to attack me while I'm in the middle of the ICU. Last time, he caught me in the hallway alone. Trust me, I won't make that mistake again." The more she thought about her agreement to keep Eagle here with her, the more upset she became.

"Okay, how about if I take Eagle back to your place, then bring him back here when your shift is over?" Isaac suggested. "That way he won't be cooped up back here, and you'll be safe."

"That would be great." She wanted to give Isaac a hug in thanks, but managed to keep herself in check. "If you're sure it's not too much of an inconvenience?"

"It's fine." He waved off her concern. "You're finished around nineteen thirty, correct?"

"Yes, but just know that sometimes I don't get out right away," she cautioned. "Patient care comes first."

"Understood. Come on, Eagle, let's get out of here." Isaac took the dog's leash and left the critical care area.

Vanessa downed a quick bite to eat, then returned to her duties. After transferring one patient to the regular floor, she was notified of an impending admission.

A short while later, the ER brought up a young man lying unresponsive on a stretcher, with a breathing tube in his airway.

"Twenty-five-year-old white male found down outside the food services loading dock," the ER nurse informed her. "Suspected drug overdose, but tox screen is pending."

Vanessa frowned at the young man. "He looks familiar."

"Not surprising. His name is Joseph Kramer and he's a civilian employee working in the housekeeping department. He often cleans right here in the ICU."

"You're right, that's exactly how I know him." Vanessa began hooking the patient up to the monitor while the respiratory therapist connected him to the ventilator.

"He's a nice guy," the ER nurse said, her expression grim. "But it's not looking good. His shift started at fourteen hundred and he wasn't found until fifteen thirty." She shrugged. "No way to know how long he was down. Illegal drugs are really creating havoc in our society these days."

True, that. Vanessa began to assess her newest patient for herself. She was forced to agree; Joe Kramer's condition was extremely serious. One of his pupils was blown, and the other wasn't very reactive upon her exam.

She quickly called the neurosurgeon to let him know of the deterioration of Joe's neurological status. As she injected the mannitol the doctor ordered to help bring down the swelling in his brain, her ex, Captain Leo Turner, strolled up to the bedside.

"Hi, Vanessa," he greeted her as if they were still on friendly terms. "I didn't hear about a new trauma patient being admitted."

She gritted her teeth and finished giving the medication. "That's because this patient isn't a trauma patient. He is being comanaged by pulmonary medicine and neurosurgery."

"What happened?" Leo asked, oblivious to her discomfort.

"Drug overdose," she admitted tersely. She dropped the syringe in the sharps container. Then she tucked her stethoscope buds into her ears, effectively shutting him out, and listened once again to her patient's breath sounds. She didn't like the way they were diminished in the bases, and wondered if her patient had aspirated while he was lying on the ground. If so, he might have pneumonia brewing.

Leo continued to stand at her patient's bedside, as if he had no place more important to be.

Unfortunately for her, the trauma bay must be quiet this evening.

When she couldn't delay any longer, she pulled the stethoscope from her ears. She moved away from the bedside, even though her patient was not awake to hear them. "Do you need anything else, Captain Turner?" she asked pointedly.

Leo met her gaze full-on. "Do you want to get together after work?" he asked. "We could head over to Carmen's for dinner."

Seriously? Was he out of his mind? Seeking her out at work? Asking her out after she'd caught him cheating on her? Talk about nerve! "No, thank you," she said politely, even though every instinct in her body wanted to rant and rave at him.

"Vanessa? Line one is the lab. They have a critical value on one of your patients."

"Excuse me." Vanessa gratefully latched onto the excuse to leave. She avoided the phone sitting on the desk near Leo in favor of taking the call at the unit secretary's desk. "This is First Lieutenant Gomez."

"We have a critical lab value on the drug screen that was sent down an hour ago on Joseph Kramer," the lab tech informed her. "The amount of Tyraxal in his blood stream is critical at four times the expected level."

"Four times the expected level," she repeated as her mind whirled.

This was now the third Tyraxal overdose in the past two weeks.

And why would a civilian janitor be taking Tyraxal anyway?

She'd already called the psychiatrist, Lieutenant Colonel Flintman, once, but he hadn't gotten back to her yet. She knew the kindly psychiatrist was busy treating patients, such as her brother, but this was important. Obviously, she needed to contact him again.

In her humble opinion, this latest and greatest PTSD medication was causing far more harm than good.

After bringing Eagle back, Isaac spent the rest of the afternoon with Aiden and the puppies. The kid really seemed to be doing great, and he hoped Vanessa's brother continued to make good progress.

Although, he knew only too well how easy it was for the nightmares to pop up out of nowhere, holding you hostage in their dark and terror-filled grip.

He did his best to broach the subject of recovering emotionally after combat with Aiden, but the kid didn't want to discuss it. Refused to even look him in the eye, so Isaac dropped the issue and focused on helping to care for the pups.

At one point, Tango stretched out between him and Aiden, and he'd noticed the young man scratching the therapy dog behind the ears a few times and smiling when Tango licked his fingers.

Hadn't Vanessa mentioned something about Aiden not connecting with the therapy dog previously assigned to him? Now that Beacon was home, maybe he could convince Westley to shift Tango's assignment to Aiden.

He made a mental note to broach the subject with the master sergeant once Kyle had discharged Beacon into his care. It would be great to know that Tango's talents would be used where they were desperately needed.

Aiden cooked a pizza for dinner and afterward, Isaac cleaned up the dishes while Aiden took the pups out for another round of housebreaking.

"Aiden, do you mind if I leave Tango here with you?" Isaac offered Tango's leash. "I need to take Eagle up to meet your sister so we can walk her home."

"That's fine," Aiden agreed. The younger man met his gaze. "Don't hurt my sister. She's been through enough."

It was on the tip of his tongue to ask exactly

what Aiden meant, but he swallowed the urge. For one thing, Vanessa should be the one to tell him if she was so inclined. And secondly, he didn't want to encourage her brother to break her trust.

"The last thing I want to do is to hurt Vanessa," Isaac said. "I'm not looking for a relationship and as far as I know, she's not, either. We're friends, okay?"

Her brother didn't look convinced. "That's what she said, too."

Ouch. That stung, more than it should considering he'd just told Aiden the same thing. He forced a smile. "See? We're both on the same page."

Isaac took the Doberman's leash, impressed at how well the dog walked calmly alongside. Considering the animal was trained to protect Vanessa, he'd expected a little trouble.

Maybe all the time they'd spent together over the past few days had smoothed things over. Eagle was already accustomed to having Isaac around.

He timed it so that he arrived at the hospital ICU right at Vanessa's quitting time. If she had to work later, that was fine; he didn't mind waiting around for her to finish.

Keeping her safe was all that mattered.

He didn't have to wait long. Ten minutes later,

Vanessa came out of the ICU, swiping at her eyes. It took a second for him to realize she'd been crying.

"What happened?" He stepped closer, eyeing her with concern. "Are you hurt?"

"No, I'm fine." Her facial expression belied her words, especially when her eyes filled with tears.

Watching her silently weep shredded his heart. There had to be something wrong, but what? He instinctively pulled her into his arms, cradling her close. He half expected her to push him away, but she didn't.

Instead, she wrapped her arms around his waist and sagged against him as if she didn't have the strength to hold herself upright.

Eagle didn't like her distress, either, and he kept shoving his nose between them, as if trying to figure out what was wrong.

Vanessa pressed her face against his chest for several minutes before she dragged in a deep breath and lifted her head. "I'm sorry for getting your shirt all wet."

"Vanessa, my shirt isn't important, but you are. Talk to me. Tell me what happened."

She sniffed and swiped at her eyes again, then absently patted Eagle's head. "I lost a patient, a young man just a few years older than Aiden."

"I'm sorry," he murmured, lightly stroking

a hand down her back. "It can't be easy to lose young patients like that."

"It's not just losing them, it's *how* we're losing them." A flash of anger glittered in her brown eyes. "He died from what the doctors are calling an accidental drug overdose."

His chest tightened as he remembered how difficult it had been not to succumb to drugs or alcohol after returning from Afghanistan. There was still the rare occasion that he was tempted to shut down the nightmares using artificial means.

"It's not easy to function when you're suffering from PTSD."

"That's just it." Vanessa tipped her head back and looked up at him with large red puffy eyes. "This is the third overdose of Tyraxal in the last two weeks, but the patient wasn't an airman or pilot who'd been in combat. He was a civilian working here in the hospital as a janitor."

He frowned. "That's odd."

"Isn't it?" Vanessa's gaze reflected her concern. "And it's worse because he shouldn't be taking PTSD meds. Makes me mad to think some guy is selling his prescription to make a few bucks."

"Maybe you should report this to Justin," he suggested.

"I will." Her shoulders slumped. "But that won't bring Joseph back. If you had seen his mother sobbing at his bedside…" Her voice trailed off and her eyes filled with fat tears. He wanted, needed, to comfort her, so he pulled her close and cradled her against his chest.

And when she lifted her head to look up at him, it took every ounce of willpower he possessed to fight the insane urge to kiss her.

SIX

Vanessa couldn't breathe, her lungs seemingly frozen as she stared into Isaac's incredible green eyes. Every sense was on alert, anticipating his kiss. When he took a step backward, releasing her, she was hit by an acute sense of loss.

She dragged in a deep breath and attempted to pull herself together. Isaac's embrace had distracted her from what really mattered. This wasn't about her growing awareness of the tall, sandy-haired and handsome combat pilot, but about the senseless death of a young man.

It was impossible to get the image of Joseph's mother sobbing at his bedside out of her mind. But she wiped the dampness off her face and squared her shoulders. The young man's death had hit hard, mostly because she kept thinking about how it would feel to lose Aiden.

There had been times she'd feared her brother would go down that dark and desperate path. Recently, Aiden seemed to be holding his own.

Therapy with the base psychiatrist and fostering the puppies were working.

"Ready to walk home?" Isaac held out Eagle's leash, which she gratefully accepted.

"Yes." There wasn't anything more she could do about Joseph Kramer's death now. She'd left another message with Lieutenant Colonel Flintman to let him know about this latest Tyraxal overdose and the fact that the patient wasn't even in the Air Force. What she really wanted to know, but doubted the lieutenant colonel would tell her, is which one of his patients might be selling his prescription on the street.

No other explanation as to how Joseph Kramer had gotten the medication made sense.

"I wonder if the Tyraxal that guy had been given was laced with some other drug?" Isaac mused as they walked along the sidewalk. "Maybe a narcotic? For all we know, it could be some concoction put together by that Olio Crime Organization Justin mentioned."

"It's possible, but I'd think that drug would have shown up on the toxicology screen, as well."

"True." Isaac rubbed the back of his neck. "I still think you need to talk to the captain."

"I will, although I may wait until morning." She frowned, suddenly realizing that only one dog was between them. "Where's Tango?"

"Oh, I left him with Aiden." Isaac offered a crooked smile. "He didn't seem to mind."

Was it possible her brother was now emotionally ready to connect with a therapy dog? She'd secretly been a little worried about what would happen when the puppies no longer needed fostering. She doubted that Aiden would be allowed to keep all four of them. She'd been hopeful that maybe her brother would be able to keep one.

Something she'd intended to keep praying for.

"I was hoping that once Kyle releases Beacon from his care, we could arrange for Tango to be reassigned to your brother. The second time might be the charm."

She smiled. "Funny, I was thinking the same thing. Either getting Tango assigned or maybe being allowed to keep one of the pups."

"Both might be good options," Isaac said. "Tango is a trained therapy dog, so he'd be able to offer Aiden support right away. Meanwhile, it's possible Westley will assign someone to show Aiden how to train the puppies, too."

She stopped for a moment and turned to face him. "That's brilliant! Aiden would absolutely love it."

"I'm happy to put in a good word for him." Isaac's low, husky voice sent ripples of awareness down her arms.

"I'd appreciate that, and so would he." With

an effort to ignore her out-of-control attraction to the man, she resumed walking. Eagle stayed close at her side. "It's highly competitive to be assigned to the dog handler program. Not sure an E-2 airman whose previous job was to do mechanic work on the fleet stands much of a chance."

"Is that what Aiden did in Afghanistan?" Isaac glanced at her curiously.

She nodded. "He doesn't like to talk about what happened, but I know that a suicide bomber was involved. A young local, barely old enough to drive, plowed directly into the fleet of parked vehicles. Aiden saw the whole thing, including the blast of the bomb and the death of his buddy."

Isaac winced. "How awful for him."

She nodded. "No worse than what you went through, I imagine."

"I flew combat for eighteen months straight, before our chopper was hit." Isaac shrugged. "I'd be dead if not for Beacon saving my life."

She rested her palm on his shoulder. His muscles tensed, so she quickly dropped her hand. They turned down Webster and seeing the veterinary clinic prodded her to ask, "How is Beacon doing? Did you visit him this morning?"

"Yeah, but unfortunately, his wound isn't looking great," Isaac admitted. "Kyle is going to switch antibiotics. If all goes well for a solid twenty-four hours, he'll consider discharging him the following morning."

"I'm glad to hear it." Vanessa felt awful about what had happened to Beacon, but she trusted Kyle Roark's instincts. If he wanted to watch Beacon longer, it was probably the right thing to do.

They approached the intersection of Webster and Viking, the corner where they'd found the puppies. She thought back, counting in her mind. Was it really just a few days ago? She shook her head in amazement.

It seemed she'd known Isaac for so much longer than that. She felt foolish for falling apart in his arms. Especially after he'd backed off, leaving an awkward silence between them. Obviously he didn't feel the same way.

Fine with her. Hadn't the debacle with Leo proven she couldn't trust her instincts around men? Was there something wrong with her that caused her to fall for men who weren't interested?

Enough of putting herself through the wringer for a man. She had her younger brother's mental health to consider. Along with staying focused on the patients she cared for.

The cop standing outside her front door gave a crisp salute as she and Isaac approached.

She and Isaac returned the acknowledgment

with salutes of their own. "Thanks for walking me home," she said, taking a step up onto the porch. "Keep me posted on how things go with Beacon."

"I will." Isaac hesitated, then added, "I need to know if you're going to talk to Justin in the morning and what time. Or have you forgotten your promise not to go anywhere alone?"

The way her pulse jumped in anticipation was ridiculous. "I didn't forget."

"Great. Then I'll swing by at zero nine hundred," Isaac said. "Good night, Vanessa."

"Good night." She stood for a moment as he turned, then called out, "Wait. You forgot Tango."

He shifted toward her. "I guess I did."

It was telling that he wasn't nearly as connected to Tango as he was to Beacon. She slipped inside with Eagle, unleashing her protector. He ignored the golden retriever, who was stretched out on the floor next to the box of puppies pressed up against the sofa where Aiden slept.

She tiptoed in an effort not to disturb the sleeping pups. Tango lifted his head at her scent, his tail hitting the floor with a muffled thump in greeting.

"Come, Tango," she whispered.

The dog rose, stretched then trotted toward

her. Eagle was slurping water from his bowl in the kitchen. She found Tango's leash, clipped it to his collar and took him outside.

"Thanks." Isaac took the strap from her hand, his fingertips lightly brushing against hers. Ignoring the tingle of awareness, she crossed her arms over her chest and stood for a moment, watching him head home.

Irrationally longing for something that could never be.

Isaac could feel Vanessa's gaze long after she disappeared inside the house.

He was losing what was left of his mind over her. He'd almost kissed her twice. And then in a rush to put distance between them, he'd almost forgotten Tango.

Yep, he was an unacceptable mess. Time to pull himself together and focus on what was important. Beacon, first and foremost, but then his career.

After Tango took care of business, he took the dog inside and glanced at the reenlistment paperwork sitting in the center of his kitchen table. It had been staring at him for days now, and he was still no closer to making a decision than he had been a week ago.

Not tonight, he told himself. Maybe he needed

to make sure Beacon was over his ordeal before he could think about the future.

He didn't sleep well, but thankfully the nightmares weren't too bad. He'd had them, but each time he'd woken up, his heart pounding, he'd instantly known that what he was seeing in his mind's eye wasn't real.

A small step in the right direction.

The following morning, he took care of Tango, showered and then made himself a full breakfast, something he didn't do on a regular basis. He'd learned the importance of eating healthy meals even when he wasn't hungry, so he forced himself to make a full breakfast twice a week.

Bacon, eggs, hash browns and a tall glass of orange juice.

He was stuffed by the time he'd finished. A glance at his watch confirmed he had thirty minutes before he was due to head over to Vanessa's, so he cleaned up his breakfast mess and washed the dishes.

Not good that he was looking forward to seeing Vanessa again, as if it had been twelve days instead of twelve hours since he last saw her. But no way was he going to renege on his promise to keep her safe. He'd just have to get over it. Besides, he found himself curious about how a civilian janitor had overdosed on a PTSD prescription medication in the first place.

He wasn't sure why being with Vanessa was so different than what he'd experienced with Amber. But now wasn't the time to examine the reasons. Instead, he clipped on Tango's leash and headed outside. The October air held a distinct chill, but he didn't mind. The leaves on the trees were still 90 percent green, the colors only just starting to change.

In another week or two, the area would be glorious. By then he would have had to make a decision about whether or not to reenlist.

Later, he told himself. He'd deal with the paperwork later. As he approached Vanessa's place, he was surprised to see she was hovering in the doorway, waiting for him. When he came up the sidewalk, she hurried down with Eagle to join him.

"Hi. Are you sure Justin cares about these drug overdoses?"

"Why wouldn't he?" He glanced at her. "If it bothers you, it's important enough to report."

"You're right." She nodded, as if to dispel her lingering doubts.

He fell into step beside her, keeping the dogs as a buffer between them.

"I notice you like to walk," she said, eyeing him curiously.

He tensed for a moment, tempted to ignore the subject, then realized as a nurse she probably already knew. "Yeah. I don't want to drive until I know I won't have a flashback."

"I see." Her brow was furrowed. "Although I'm not sure how you'll know one way or the other until you try it."

She had a point; in fact, Flintman had encouraged him to drive, as well. "Maybe."

The walk to the Base Command took almost twenty minutes as the offices were on the opposite side of the base. When they arrived, they were shown into a large office and instructed to wait for Captain Blackwood.

"I hope that means there's news on the investigation," Vanessa said in a low tone. "We really need to capture Boyd before he can harm anyone else."

"I'm surprised the blatant note from the blogger hasn't spurred some sort of retaliation by now." Isaac shook his head. "Stupid move, taunting a killer like that."

"Maybe that's partially what Justin is working on," she agreed. "They're having enough trouble finding the guy without other people meddling in the investigation."

Fifteen minutes later, Justin and his K-9, Quinn, strode in. "Sorry to keep you both waiting. Please, have a seat," he said after they'd saluted.

"Not a problem." Vanessa dropped into the

seat closest to the window, leaving him with his back to the door.

He didn't like it, but tried to ignore the weird paranoia that plagued him.

"Any news on Boyd?" Vanessa asked.

Justin's expression was grim. "Unfortunately not. I've had cops scouring the base from one side to the other, but no one has seen him." He paused, then added, "Or admitted to seeing him."

Vanessa leaned forward in her seat. "I have a concern about several drug overdoses that I've seen in the past two weeks. Three in total, and this last death was a civilian."

Justin's brows levered upward. "A civilian from where? How did he get on base?"

"He works as a janitor at the hospital. A better question is, how did a civilian noncombatant get ahold of the prescription PTSD medication known as Tyraxal?"

Justin stared at her for a long moment. "That is a good question. What are your thoughts?"

"I can only speculate that one of our airmen has sold his prescription. Tyraxal offers great benefits, but it's also highly addictive." Vanessa glanced at Isaac for a moment, and he figured she was speculating about whether or not he'd ever taken Tyraxal.

He hadn't.

"Have you shared your concerns with Lieutenant Colonel Flintman?" Justin asked with a frown.

"I have, yes," Vanessa nodded. "I'm hoping he'll get back to me today."

"Why are you bringing this issue to me?" Justin asked, sitting back in his seat.

Isaac picked up the thread. "You mentioned the Olio Crime Organization when we found the puppies. Isn't it possible they're dabbling in drugs, too?"

"You're assuming they aren't already up to their ears in dealing illegal drugs," Justin said drily. "They're likely involved in all kinds of criminal enterprises, but three overdoses involving a PTSD drug?" He grimaced. "Not sure how that would fit in with their master plan."

"You're assuming they have a master plan," Isaac joked. Then he turned somber. "Seriously, isn't it possible they're branching out? We believe they may have targeted the base by stealing four highly valuable dogs. Why not try to sneak their greedy tentacles inside this way, too?"

Justin nodded thoughtfully. "You have a point, Isaac. I can't afford to ignore any potential link to the Olio Crime Organization." He turned toward Vanessa. "Keep your eyes open at the hospital, okay? There may be other overdoses that were treated on days you weren't working that you're not even aware of."

"I know. I've already considered that." Her expression was troubled. "The thought of there being even more…" She swallowed hard.

The urge to comfort her was strong, but Isaac curled his fingers into the palms of his hands and stayed where he was. Because next time, he might not find the strength to keep himself from kissing her.

"Anything else?" Justin asked, looking a bit impatient.

"No, sir." Vanessa pushed to her feet. "Thanks for your time."

"I always appreciate being kept in the loop," Justin said. "Don't hesitate to contact me if you find other anomalies."

"Of course," she agreed.

Isaac stood and turned toward the door, feeling the muscles in his back and neck relax as his tension eased. No one was watching them or hovering outside the office doorway.

Tango wagged his tail, and he bent to scratch the golden between his ears. The dog wasn't Beacon, but he was a good companion nonetheless.

Vanessa and Eagle led the way outside. As they walked back toward Canyon Drive, he caught a glimpse of the Winged Java. "Care for a coffee?"

She looked surprised and he mentally kicked himself for not thinking before he spoke. Hadn't he decided that spending time with Vanessa wasn't smart? So why ask her to share coffee?

There was a pause before she finally nodded. "Sure, that would be great."

He wasn't disappointed in her response, which only proved how far gone he was.

The café wasn't far and the tables outside were surprisingly empty.

"I'll buy this time," she offered.

It was the perfect way to put his impulsive invitation back on friendship terms, but he couldn't do it. People could call him a chauvinist if they wanted, but he wasn't going to allow a woman to buy him coffee. Especially not since he'd invited her.

"I'll take care of it. You want an iced decaf or would you rather go for the full load of caffeine?"

"Full load, please." She plopped down in the same seat they'd used yesterday, looking exhausted, as if she hadn't slept well. No doubt she'd been upset about losing her patient to a drug overdose.

"Hang on to Tango for a minute, would you?" He handed her the golden's leash, then headed inside the café. He took his place in line and after a few minutes placed their order. As he waited, he tried to think of a way to broach the subject of their friendship.

By the time their coffee was ready, he still hadn't figured out how to bring it up without looking or sounding like an idiot.

He carried the coffee outside and couldn't help but smile when he found Vanessa speaking to both Tango and Eagle as if they were her kids.

Don't go there, he warned himself. They weren't dating, weren't a couple and no way was he going to fall in love, get married and have kids.

He couldn't even be a combat pilot anymore, so what did he have to offer Vanessa? Or any woman for that matter?

Absolutely nothing.

He dropped into the seat next to her and set her coffee down. "Talk to the dogs often?"

She flashed a brilliant smile. "Of course, and don't act as if you don't do the same thing. I've watched you with Beacon, remember?"

"Guilty as charged," he agreed. "But that's just because for three solid days Beacon and I were alone on the mountain and he was the only one I could talk to."

"Oh, Isaac." Vanessa's gaze was full of sympathy. "It breaks my heart when you say things like that."

It was the truth, but before he could say anything more, a sharp retort rang out and it took him a split second to realize that the sound was gunfire.

"Get down!" He lunged forward, grabbing Vanessa's arm and dragging her to the ground, using the table for cover.

People nearby screamed and ran, while he did his best to cover Vanessa's body with his. The sound of panic hit hard, and his vision blurred as nightmares from the past threatened to drag him into the dark abyss.

SEVEN

Vanessa couldn't believe it was happening again. The situation outside the Winged Java was eerily similar to the events that had transpired during Beacon's homecoming.

The wail of sirens indicated help was on the way. She tried to ease away from Isaac's bulky frame, but he clamped his arms around her, keeping her in place.

"So much blood," he whispered.

Blood? Where? Vanessa, scanned the area around them, but didn't see any evidence of injury. She didn't think she'd been hit, but maybe Isaac had? She squirmed again, trying to get a good look at him. The vacant expression in Isaac's eyes reminded her too much of how Aiden looked after a flashback.

"Isaac? Are you hurt?" She prayed her voice would get through to him.

He didn't answer.

"Isaac?" She shook his arm. "The cops are on the way. Are you hurt?"

"No, I'm fine." His voice was a bit stilted, but at least he'd answered. But he didn't move from beneath the table until the Security Forces cops swarmed the area. "You okay?"

"I'm fine," she assured him when they finally crawled out from beneath the table.

"Good." His color was back, although she could still see beads of sweat dotting his brow. Because of the close call? Or his flashback?

"What happened?" Justin Blackwood pushed his way through the cops.

"We were sitting and talking, when suddenly I heard gunfire," Isaac reported. "The shot came from the east."

"The training center?" Vanessa frowned. "You think it was a random shot?"

"No way." Justin swept his gaze across the area, then stepped closer to the table. The top of the umbrella had an oddly shaped hole in it. "The bullet went through here."

"Seems strange, unless someone was standing up on higher ground?" Isaac asked.

Higher ground? Vanessa looked over her shoulder. The hospital was a five-story building not far from the training center. "Are you sure the bullet came from that way?"

"I'm sure." Isaac looked at Justin, who nodded in agreement.

"I concur. It makes sense based on the trajectory."

Vanessa shivered, despite the warmth of the sun. "I guess this proves I was the target before, on the tarmac, too."

"It looks that way," Justin agreed. "Did either of you notice anything else? Anyone or anything out of the ordinary?"

"No." Vanessa felt guilty that she hadn't paid more attention to her surroundings.

Isaac's phone rang, and his gaze widened in alarm when he answered it. "Are you sure? Okay, I'll be right there."

Vanessa put a hand on Isaac's arm. "Who was that?"

"Kyle Roark. Beacon has had a setback. Apparently he's suffered a small intracranial bleed."

"Oh, Isaac. I'm sorry."

"Yeah." He stared at the phone for a moment, before slipping it into his pocket. "Kyle still thinks he'll be okay."

"Try not to worry," she said, putting her arm around his waist in a half hug. She hated feeling so helpless. "Captain Roark is a great vet. We can take comfort in knowing Beacon is in good hands."

Isaac didn't say anything in response and she

suspected he wouldn't feel whole until he had Beacon home with him.

After a few seconds, Isaac pulled away. "Thanks," he said in a gruff voice. "Justin, would you have a cop take Vanessa home? I need to head to the veterinary clinic."

"Wait, I'd rather come with you." Vanessa hated the idea of Isaac going alone.

He'd helped save her life, not just a few days ago, but now. The least she could do in return was stick by him through this added complication.

"It's not safe," Isaac protested.

She knew he was right but didn't like it. She spun around to face Justin. "Does this recent attempt mean I can't go anywhere in public? What am I supposed to do, sit home day after day? And what about my job?"

Justin let out a heavy sigh. "Okay, listen. For now, let's take added precautions. How about if I have a cop escort you both to the clinic and then home? He can hang out with you for a while, too. Will that work?"

She glanced at Isaac, who shrugged. "I won't argue."

"Works for me, too."

"Good." Justin gestured for one of the cops to join them. "Senior Airman Wade will accompany you to the vet and then see that you both get safely home."

"Thank you," Vanessa said.

The three of them were silent as they covered the short distance to the veterinary clinic. Senior Airman Wade held the door open for them, then stood off to the side so they could approach the front desk. Airman Fielding, Kyle's assistant, looked up as they entered.

"Captain Goddard? Captain Roark told me to expect you." She flashed a brief smile. "I'll let him know you're here."

Isaac stood stiff and straight at her side, his expression tense as if he were mentally preparing himself for battle rather than visiting his injured dog.

Maybe to him, it felt like the same thing. Especially after the recent gunfire.

She wondered if he was a believer and able to lean on his faith at times like this. Thinking back, she remembered how he'd said Amen after her premeal prayer, but since then he hadn't mentioned anything more about his faith or believing in God. Was it just because he didn't like to talk about something so private? Some worshipers were like that.

Please, Lord, look after Isaac's physical and mental well-being.

"Captain Goddard? You can follow me to room three," Airman Fielding announced.

"Let's go." She took Tango's leash from his fingers, keeping Tango on her left and Eagle on her right. Isaac strode past her into the exam room, where Kyle waited with Beacon on the stainless-steel table. She followed him inside, hovering at the back of the room, each dog sitting obediently at her side. Beacon wasn't as alert as the last time she'd seen him, but he thumped his tail in recognition when he caught Isaac's scent. Isaac crossed over and bent over the dog, awkwardly hugging him and whispering in his ear.

She met Kyle Roark's gaze and they shared a brief, sympathetic understanding of what Isaac was going through. Beacon had to make it through this, he just had to.

Isaac finally stepped away from the exam table. "You'll let me know if there are any changes?" His voice was low and hoarse.

"Of course. I promise to keep a close eye on him," the vet assured him.

"Thanks." Isaac turned away, his expression tortured. He moved past her as if she wasn't there, heading into the clinic lobby.

Vanessa hurried after him, still holding both dogs. Isaac nodded to Senior Airman Wade, then turned toward Vanessa. "It's time for us to get you safely home."

The reminder of how danger followed her like a shadow made her frown. She hated the thought of living in fear.

"I have an idea, Isaac," she said as the two men flanked her on either side. "You could stay at my house for a bit, to help Aiden with the puppies." The small bundles of fur helped keep her brother grounded, so it made sense that they might be able to offer some solace to Isaac, too.

He didn't respond.

"Aiden has a therapy appointment tomorrow and wants to be sure I can manage the puppies on my own for a while, so he wants to go through everything with me tonight," she added. "Apparently, he doesn't trust me to handle them for a full hour. Maybe you could stick around to help."

Isaac finally shrugged. "Sure. I'll stay until the Security Forces cop arrives at nineteen hundred."

She refused to let his less-than-enthusiastic response bother her. At least he wasn't going to sit home alone, waiting for news. What else could she say to him that would offer hope about Beacon's ability to pull through this latest setback? She had no idea.

Senior Airman Wade cleared his throat. "My

orders are to stay on duty at First Lieutenant Gomez's home for as long as she wants or until the night shift arrives."

"Glad to hear it," Isaac said.

Vanessa had the impression Isaac was relieved he had an excuse not to stay. Maybe the puppies would change his mind.

As they approached her house, they found Aiden knee-deep in another housebreaking session. There was a large square of newspaper stretched out on the grass, where the puppies were encouraged to do their business.

"Hey," Aiden greeted them distractedly. Vanessa was relieved that her brother seemed unaffected by the sound of the gunshot just a half mile away. "I think they're finally starting to get the hang of this."

"That's great news." Vanessa unleashed Eagle and watched as the Doberman went over to sniff at the puppies. No easy task as they left the newspaper to romp around the yard, keeping Aiden busy chasing after them. Her brother must have been frustrated, but she was impressed by Aiden's good-natured humor about the whole thing.

"I'm planning to feed them more mash," Aiden warned. "But don't worry, I'll use the bathtub trick again."

"Good idea. Stick with something that works," she agreed.

Her brother apparently just noticed the Security Forces cop standing near the front door. "What's up with the guard?"

"Oh, well…" She hesitated, then remembered her promise not to lie to her brother. "There was another gunshot near the Winged Java, so I've been offered additional protection."

Aiden's gaze widened in alarm. "You're okay?" He glanced at Isaac then back at her. "Both of you are all right?"

"We're fine," she reassured him. "But it's best to take the puppies inside now, just to be safe."

Isaac chased one determined pup, Denali based on the notch in her right ear, scooping her up before she hit the sidewalk and cuddling her close for a moment before returning her to the cardboard box in the middle of the yard.

Just when she thought maybe the puppies were beginning to help soothe his frayed nerves, Isaac abruptly turned away. "You should get them inside. I'm heading home."

"Wait!" She rushed to his side. "Are you sure it's a good idea for you to be alone right now?"

He avoided her gaze and shrugged. "I have Tango."

Tango was a good therapy dog, but Isaac had already confided in her that he didn't have a connection with the golden the way he did with Beacon.

"Please stay."

"I can't."

She couldn't force him, as much as she wanted to. Finally, she relented. "I'll keep you and Beacon in my prayers, Isaac," she softly promised.

He let out a harsh sound. "Don't bother. God hasn't listened to me in a long time. I doubt He'll start now."

"Isaac..." Her heart ached for him, but he didn't acknowledge her as he walked away.

She stood long after he was gone, wondering what she could do to help the man who'd turned his back on his faith.

"What's with him?" Aiden's voice broke into her thoughts.

"Isaac is upset because Beacon had a setback."

Aiden winced. "I'm sorry to hear that."

"Me, too." Since there wasn't anything more she could do for Isaac at the moment, she walked back toward Aiden, picking up Shenandoah before she could leave the yard. "Okay, let's go inside so you can show me what I need to do to care for them."

Safely inside the house, with the cop stationed outside, Aiden went into a detailed description of what he'd been doing to care for the pups, but she was only half listening.

Deep down, she couldn't tear her mind away from Isaac's suffering. Or the implication of the most recent attempt to harm her.

Sunday church services were only three days away. She was scheduled for a twelve-hour shift on Saturday, but thankfully had tomorrow, which was Friday, off, and again on Sunday.

Her safety was in God's hands and those of the cop stationed outside her door. She could pray for Isaac, but longed to do more. Maybe Pastor Harmon had something to offer. The man had an uncanny way of knowing just what his parishioners needed to hear.

But for that to be successful, she needed to convince Isaac to accompany her to the service.

Based on this most recent interaction, she was afraid that might be an impossible task.

Isaac stared blindly out the window at his small backyard, battling a feeling of emptiness. He knew that sitting in his house alone wasn't smart. But he hadn't been able to stay at Vanessa's, either. He told himself he wasn't betraying his promise to keep her safe, because the task had been handed over to Senior Airman Wade.

Besides, watching the puppies play had only

reminded him of the gap left behind in Beacon's absence. Logically, he knew the dog was getting the best care possible by Kyle Roark, but that didn't mean he liked being here without him.

The reckless gunman, likely Boyd Sullivan, was responsible for Beacon's injury. And he had taken a second shot at Vanessa. He knew Justin was determined to get the guy, but he wanted to help.

Restless, he rose to his feet, wishing he could find a way to track down Boyd Sullivan. Not that he thought he could manage to accomplish what Justin Blackwood's team had been unable to do.

He paced, and when that didn't work, he clipped a leash onto Tango's collar and headed back outside. In the past, walking around the base had helped keep him focused.

Steering clear of Vanessa's, he walked past the church, his steps slowed as Vanessa's words echoed in his memory.

I'll keep you and Beacon in my prayers, Isaac.

For a moment, he regretted his harsh response. He'd only spoken the truth, but the shocked expression on Vanessa's face confirmed he'd been too blunt about it.

He hadn't attended church services since he'd been back on base. When he and Beacon had been stranded on the mountain in Afghanistan, he'd prayed day and night for rescue. And the search and recover team had eventually found them. He'd thanked God for that, but in the ensuing months, as he'd been plagued by nightmares while unable to get Beacon returned to him, his faith had vanished.

His career was in shambles and Beacon had been injured by a nutjob with a gun.

Where was God now?

With resolute determination, he strode past the church. He didn't have a destination in mind as he walked past the officers' club and the airmen training facilities. When he reached the helipad, he stared at the choppers for a moment, mourning the loss of his career, then turned and headed past the hangar to Canyon Drive.

He walked in a circle around the base, eventually returning to his house.

Tango had willingly kept pace with him as he walked for miles and miles. When he returned home, Isaac felt bad for him and made sure to provide the golden with plenty of food and water, along with a special doggy treat. Isaac wasn't hungry, but forced himself to eat a grilled cheese sandwich that tasted like cardboard.

After dinner, he stretched out on the sofa, exhaustion weighing him down. Tango stretched out on the floor beside him, but he barely noticed.

* * *

"Delta one-five, do you read me, over?"

Isaac could barely hear their command center over the rat-a-tat-tat of gunfire.

"Delta one-five, what's your twenty?"

The bird jerked beneath the stick and it was all Isaac could do to keep the chopper airborne. "This is Delta one-five, we are under heavy artillery fire. Repeat, we are under fire!"

A bullet found its mark and the chopper tilted sideways, sending his passenger and best friend, Jake Burke, and his K-9, Beacon, slamming into the side of the bird.

Sweat rolled down his face beneath his helmet, and he held on to the stick with every ounce of strength he possessed, doing everything possible to keep the chopper in the air, while his copilot had been keeping track of their location.

"Mayday, Mayday. We're hit." He squinted at the landscape below, desperate for a place to land. "Repeat, we're hit. I'm going down."

There! He glimpsed a small field and aimed the nose of the chopper in that direction. Another jerk as the bird took more gunfire.

Then they were falling, falling…landing with a jarring thud. A tree branch had poked through the window, piercing his copilot in the chest. Isaac yanked off his safety harness and checked for a pulse, but found nothing. Then he scrambled back to check on Jake and Beacon.

Beacon stood protectively near his handler. Jake's chest was *covered* in blood. Isaac ripped off his helmet, intending to do CPR, silently screaming when he realized his efforts were futile. The chopper jerked again and a large explosion filled the air. He saw the bright ball of flames shooting from the engine, seconds before the force sent him reeling backward.

He saw Jake's lifeless eyes…then nothing but darkness.

Noooo!

Isaac awoke to a sore, hoarse throat and the sound of his own screams. Tango whimpered, his paws on his chest, attempting to lick his face.

For a moment, he gathered the golden close, burying his face against Tango's glossy coat. His heart pounded in rhythm with the rat-a-tat-tat of gunfire that continued to echo through his memory.

He lifted his head, and pressed a hand to the center of his chest in an effort to slow his pulse. It had been months since he'd had this particular nightmare. Lately, he'd managed to wake himself up before the crash landing.

Before he gazed first into his copilot's slack face and then Jake's lifeless blue eyes.

Feeling shaky, he gently moved Tango to the side so he could get up off the sofa. He padded into the kitchen and downed a glass of water, willing himself to stop trembling.

He knew it was ridiculous to have this kind of response to a nightmare. Especially over something that had happened six months ago.

The clock on the microwave read zero one thirty. The need to see Vanessa was strong, and he tamped it back with an effort.

No sense in waking her up in the middle of the night, especially since he had no clue if she was scheduled to work the next day or not.

Again, he paced the length of the house, unable to release the nightmare's grip on his subconscious. Later, when he closed his eyes, he found himself right back in the cockpit, fighting to keep the bird in the air.

While Jake lay bleeding to death right behind him.

Enough. He couldn't stay inside the house a moment longer. Sitting here alone wasn't going to work. He needed to get out. He glanced down at Tango. "How about it, boy? Up to taking a walk?"

Tango wagged his tail.

After clipping a leash to Tango's collar, he headed outside, breathing deep. The cool night air provided a balm for his ragged nerves. He instinctively turned toward Vanessa's house. He wouldn't bother her, but would walk past, make sure things were fine.

Aiden might be having trouble sleeping, too. Lots of combat veterans suffering from PTSD didn't sleep through the night. Maybe if Aiden was awake, they could talk for a bit. He knew Vanessa wanted her brother to open up to him.

But when he approached her home, the hairs on the back of his neck stood on end and a wave of apprehension washed over him. As he came closer, he could see a body lying in a crumpled heap against the side of the house.

The cop stationed outside her door was injured!

He bolted forward, leaning down to feel for a pulse along the side of his neck. The beat of the cop's heart was reassuring despite the thin trail of blood that ran down the side of his temple.

Vanessa!

His heart lodged in his throat as he rushed through the front door hanging ajar, the frame cracked from where it had been forced open. He hurried, hoping and desperately praying that he wasn't too late and that Vanessa wasn't already dead at Boyd's hand.

Why hadn't he brought his phone? He wanted to kick himself for not being better prepared.

He swept his gaze over the darkened interior

of the house, searching for signs of an intruder. The TV was still in the corner, and he noticed a laptop sitting on an end table. Clearly, robbery wasn't the motive.

Moving silently and with extreme caution, he made his way through the living room, toward the kitchen. He wished he'd grabbed the injured cop's duty weapon.

A masked man stood near the back door, holding a cardboard box awkwardly against his chest. Even from where Isaac stood several feet away, he could hear a whimpering sound inside.

The intruder had grabbed the puppies? Why? "Hey! Stop!"

The masked man jerked at the sound of Isaac's voice. Isaac lunged toward the guy at the exact same time the intruder threw the box of puppies at him and pulled out a knife.

Isaac instinctively caught the box, risking a quick glance inside to see that the four puppies were okay. He set the box on the floor and confronted the masked man, his combat training instinctively kicking in. He settled in a fighting stance keeping his arms loose at his side. Without warning, he abruptly lashed out with his booted foot, aiming squarely for the wrist holding the knife.

The blade clattered to the floor.

His surge of satisfaction faded as the intruder

immediately turned and escaped through the back door.

Isaac took off after him. No way was he letting Boyd Sullivan get away!

The guy was smart, taking a zigzag path through the trees and leaping over bushes. Isaac easily kept pace, and pushed himself to close the gap between them.

Boyd would not get away!

The masked man glanced over his shoulder in time to see Isaac closing in. He instantly changed directions, running directly out onto the two-lane road leading toward the south gate.

Isaac didn't slow his pace, hoping the cop on duty at the gate would see the masked man, too. A sudden squeal of brakes shattered the night, followed by a loud thump-thump.

Stumbling into the clearing, he stared in horror at the body of the masked man lying off to the side of the road in a boneless heap.

The truck driver slid out from behind the wheel. "He came out of nowhere, running right in front of me! I couldn't stop!"

"I know, it's okay." Isaac crossed over and checked for a pulse.

Nothing. The man was dead. Just like Jake.

No, don't go there. He gave himself a mental shake and looked up at the driver, who was on the phone with the cops.

Isaac hesitated, then reached down to remove the mask. He'd expected to see a familiar face staring up at him.

But the dead man wasn't Boyd Sullivan. He was someone Isaac had never seen before.

EIGHT

The sound of a shout followed by several loud thuds brought Vanessa out of a dead sleep. Worried about her brother, she ran into the main living area, searching wildly for Aiden.

He was crouched next to the box of puppies on the floor, attempting to soothe them.

"What happened?" she asked.

"I came out of my room to see Isaac running outside and the box sitting in the middle of the kitchen." Aiden's gaze was troubled. "I left the puppies in the living room when I went to bed and can't see why Isaac would move them."

Vanessa didn't understand it, either. Why would Isaac have been there? She heard a moan from the front of the house and quickly responded. When she saw the cop propped against the side of her house, she dropped to her knees, her nursing training rising to the forefront. "Senior Airman McDonald, are you okay?"

"Someone hit me." The cop touched the right

side of his temple with a wince. "I'm sorry, ma'am. I shouldn't have been caught unaware."

"It's not your fault." Vanessa glanced around her front yard, shivering in the cool night. Then she focused on the injured cop. "How long were you unconscious?"

He shrugged his shoulders. "No idea."

She didn't like being out in the open like this. What if Boyd Sullivan or his accomplice was out there watching them right now? "Let's get you inside, okay? I'll call for an ambulance."

"I need to contact my captain." Senior Airman McDonald didn't look happy with the idea of reporting in. It probably wouldn't be easy to admit someone had sneaked up on him, knocking him unconscious. "He needs to know what happened here."

She couldn't disagree. And where was Isaac? Aiden saw him running away. Had he chased the intruder? Was it possible he'd already caught Boyd?

She hoped and prayed he had.

Propping her shoulder beneath McDonald's arm, she helped him upright. As they made their way inside, Isaac rushed through the house, stopping abruptly when he saw her, relief filling his eyes.

"I'm glad you're okay," he said. "Can I borrow

your phone? I left mine behind, and we need to contact Captain Blackwood ASAP."

She assisted McDonald into a kitchen chair, then went into her bedroom to fetch the mobile phone she routinely charged at night.

She wasn't sure why Isaac had shown up in the middle of the night, but was grateful for his impeccable timing.

"Here." She handed him the phone. "What happened? Did you catch the man who hit the senior airman?"

Isaac shook his head. "I chased him, but he ran out onto the street directly in the path of a truck. I think he hoped to get past it as a way to lose me, but his plan didn't work." He hesitated, then added, "He's dead."

"Boyd is dead?" she repeated, torn between horror and relief that the nightmare might be over.

"Not Boyd," Isaac corrected. "Some guy I never saw before in my life."

"What?" Vanessa didn't understand.

"He was trying to steal the puppies. He threw the box at me, then pulled a knife. I managed to disarm him, and when he took off, I chased him."

"He hit a cop to steal puppies?" The whole scenario didn't make any sense.

"I don't understand it, either." Isaac turned

away and spoke into the phone. "Justin? You need to come to Vanessa's place. It's an active crime scene."

Vanessa couldn't hear the other side of the conversation, so she focused on the cop. She pulled a bag of frozen peas out and handed it to McDonald. "Use this as an ice pack."

He gratefully accepted the frozen peas, pressing the bag to his temple.

She peered into his eyes, assessing his pupils. They looked equal and reactive to light. "Do you feel dizzy? Confused? Sick to your stomach?"

"I have a headache, that's all."

She wasn't sure she believed him; Security Forces cops didn't like to admit to weakness. "Don't lie to me, Senior Airman," she warned. "Head injuries are no joke. You could die from bleeding into your brain."

He stared at her for a moment, then admitted, "A little dizzy and sick, but nothing serious."

That's all she needed to know. "Fine. I recommend you go to the emergency room for a CT scan."

McDonald didn't argue, which only convinced her he was hurting far more than he'd let on. She glanced at Aiden, who was trying to hold all four puppies in his arms at the same time, his expression laden with guilt.

"They're okay, Aiden." She placed a reassuring hand on her brother's shoulder.

"I should have either slept on the sofa the way I usually do, or taken them into the bedroom with me," Aiden said.

"It's not your fault."

"I almost lost them!" Aiden's voice rose in agitation. "Isaac said that man tried to steal them away from us. Who would do such an awful thing?"

"I don't know." Vanessa couldn't make sense out of any of it. "What matters now is that the puppies are safe, and Senior Airman McDonald will be okay, too."

Unfortunately, the masked man was dead.

If not Boyd, then who was he? And why did he want the puppies?

Justin Blackwood and his K-9, Quinn, along with two more cops, arrived at the same time as the ambulance. Vanessa gave a brief update to the medics about McDonald's condition and then stepped back so they could get him to the hospital. Then she crossed over to join Justin and Isaac.

"You just happened to be walking by Vanessa's house and noticed the injured officer?" Justin asked in an incredulous tone.

"Yes." Isaac met his gaze squarely. "If you

must know, I had a nightmare and couldn't sleep. I decided a walk would help clear my head."

"Without your phone?" Justin pressed, clearly upset with how the situation had been handled.

Vanessa instinctively moved closer to Isaac.

"Yes, without my phone. The nightmare knocked me off balance. It was a stupid move. I should have been better prepared."

"Isaac isn't the bad guy here," she pointed out.

"I know." Justin let out a heavy sigh. "Go on. You were walking past Vanessa's house when you noticed the injured cop. You didn't have a phone so you made sure he was breathing, then went inside."

"I needed to make sure Vanessa and Aiden were okay." Isaac glanced at her, then continued with the story about how the intruder was near the back door, holding the box of puppies.

"Why would he take the puppies?" Justin demanded. "A shot at you earlier, then this? It doesn't make sense."

"I know," Vanessa admitted.

"It's definitely weird. When he saw me, he threw the box and pulled a knife. I disarmed him, and he took off running." Isaac hesitated, then shrugged. "I thought it was Boyd, so I kept after him. Then he tried to cross the road in front of the truck, I assume in an attempt to lose me. But he was hit instead. I believe he must have broken his neck on impact." The words were carefully articulated and she sensed it wasn't easy for him to talk about this. "I removed his mask and confirmed he wasn't Boyd Sullivan."

"Who was he?" Justin asked.

"Some guy I've never seen before."

"Walk us through the path you took," Justin ordered taking Quinn by the leash and stepping forward.

Vanessa didn't want to leave Aiden alone, but there were two cops standing by, so she pulled on a rumpled Air Force sweatshirt emblazoned with the motto "Aim High, Fly, Fight, Win" and followed Isaac and Justin outside.

The masked intruder had taken a jagged path through the base neighborhood and when they emerged from the trees, she saw the truck sitting in the center of the road, the apparent driver speaking to a couple of cops she assumed had come over from the south gate.

An ambulance stood by, waiting for direction. There was obviously no rush to remove the deceased man. Vanessa had the distinct urge to verify for herself that it wasn't Boyd lying there.

It wasn't.

And like Isaac, she'd never seen this man before in her life.

"I don't recognize him," Justin said thoughtfully. "We'll need his fingerprints to verify he's not military."

"Can we take him to the morgue?" one of the medics asked.

Justin examined the front of the semitruck, likely making note of the new dent. The two cops from the south gate crossed over to join them, greeting the officers with a sharp salute.

"Did you see what happened?" Justin asked.

"Yes, sir." The airman first class named Steele stepped forward. "I caught a glimpse of a man running into the road in front of the truck. The semitruck couldn't stop in time and made contact with the pedestrian. He flew up in the air and landed at the side of the road on his head."

The airman first class's account validated Isaac's statement, so Justin gestured at the medic. "Go ahead and take him to the morgue." Then he turned toward Airman First Class Steele. "I want to see your report first thing in the morning."

"Yes, sir." The airman first class saluted again, then turned away.

Vanessa glanced between Isaac and Justin. "Is it possible this could be linked to the missing dogs and the Olio Crime Organization?"

"I don't see how," Justin admitted.

"I stand by my earlier theory," Isaac said. "I believe it's possible members of the Olio Crime Organization are attempting to infiltrate Canyon

Air Force Base. Maybe they returned to steal the puppies back?"

"Why would they?" Justin countered. "What value is there to the puppies? Besides, why try to infiltrate the base at all? There are easier places, dozens of other cities in the area, in which to organize crime."

"Maybe it's military related," Vanessa pressed. She was sure there was something else going on, something other than Boyd's killing spree, which really was bad enough. "You must know something about what they're involved in."

Justin hesitated, shrugged. "I'm really not at liberty to say. Base Command hasn't given me clearance to discuss it."

Vanessa tried not to show her impatience. "This masked man attacked a cop, broke into my home and tried to steal four puppies, and you're not allowed to discuss it with me?"

Isaac put a reassuring hand on her arm. "He's just following orders."

Vanessa had been in the Air Force for six years, going in right after she'd graduated from a four-year nursing program. She knew that the command structure was hierarchical and teams often worked in silos. But this issue impacted her on a personal level.

Shouldn't that count for something?

"You brought me in when I received a red rose

from Boyd. I've been attacked twice, maybe a third time if you assume I was the shooter's victim at the airfield the other day. Why shut me out now?"

Justin's expression was noncommittal. "I'll discuss your concerns with our Base Commander Lieutenant General Hall."

Great. That would help about as much as placing a bandage over a brisk arterial bleed. Isaac's arm slid around her waist and he steered her away from Justin and Quinn, back toward her house.

She leaned against Isaac, grateful for his support. When they were out of Justin's earshot, she glanced up at him. "I'm glad you were there to protect us."

Isaac gently hugged her. "Me, too."

It was scary how much she was coming to depend on Isaac. And how much she cared about him on a personal level.

Keeping their relationship on friendship terms felt impossible.

Despite being burned in the past by Leo, she wanted more. Much more.

Isaac paused outside Vanessa's back door, fighting the urge to kiss her.

Not just because he was relieved to find her safe and sound, but because he needed her.

Yet at the same time, it wasn't easy to trust his instincts. These circumstances were anything but normal, and he knew that feelings were amplified in crisis situations.

He was grateful to have been able to prevent her from being harmed yet again. When he'd thought she might be lying inside the house, injured or worse, he'd prayed to God that he'd find her in time.

Praying had felt right, and it occurred to him that maybe he'd been wrong to shy away from his faith.

Maybe God was watching over them.

The thought brought him a sense of peace.

"I'm so glad the puppies are safe," Vanessa said, flashing a relieved smile. "Losing them would have been a huge setback for Aiden."

"I know. Just like Beacon's head injury has set me back." Was that why the nightmare had returned with such vengeance? It was as if he'd been right there, living the experience all over again. "I think that's why I was plagued by a recurring nightmare tonight."

"Oh, Isaac, I'm sorry about Beacon and your nightmare, but thank you so much for arriving in time." Vanessa lifted up on her tiptoes and brushed his rough cheek with a light kiss. Before he could haul her into his arms for a proper kiss, she moved away and went through the back door into the kitchen.

He followed her inside and found Aiden corralling the puppies from the wet newspaper. The young man glanced up at his sister with a hesitant smile. "Even as scared as they were, they didn't make a mess in the box."

"I'm glad to hear it." Vanessa helped dispose of the soiled newspaper and then washed her hands at the sink as her brother followed suit.

"Aiden, will it bother you too much if I camp out on the sofa for what's left of the night?" Isaac asked. "I don't want to leave you and your sister alone."

"I don't mind." Aiden tightened his grip on the box. "But the puppies are staying in my room with me."

"Understandable," Isaac agreed. "I don't want to make you uncomfortable, either."

Aiden glanced at his sister, then back at Isaac. "I'd feel better having someone to protect us here, inside the house," he said frankly. "It's obvious having a cop stationed outside isn't good enough."

Isaac silently agreed, although he suspected Justin would take issue with the young man's assessment. "Great, thanks."

Aiden nodded and headed down the short hallway to his bedroom, disappearing inside.

"That's settled," Vanessa said. "I'll find a spare blanket and pillow."

Before he could tell her not to bother, she left him alone in the kitchen. He crossed over to the adjacent living room, and stood for a moment, feeling uncertain.

Every cell in his body wanted to stick close to Vanessa after everything that had transpired, but deep down, he knew staying here wasn't smart. He was already too close to the edge, desperate to move beyond friendship, seeking something more.

He scrubbed his hands over his face, weary of trying to make sense out of his feelings. Emotions weren't logical, so there was no point in trying to dissect and analyze them.

"Here you go." Vanessa returned with a light blanket and a pillow, setting them both in the corner of the sofa. He stared at the flowered pillowcase, wondering if it smelled like her.

If that was the case, he'd never get any sleep. Not that he was expecting much shut-eye anyway.

"Thanks," he said. "You should try to get some rest, especially if you work in the morning." Glancing at the time—nearly zero three hundred hours—he winced. "In a few hours, I mean."

"I don't, but am scheduled on Saturday." She

hesitated, then added, "I'm off Sunday, too. I was—um—thinking, or um, hoping, you'd consider joining me and Aiden at church services. I don't know if you've heard Pastor Harmon speak, but he does an amazing job."

His initial instinct was to refuse. It had been too long since he'd crossed the threshold of a church, much less found solace in one. But remembering his promise to protect her, he nodded in agreement. "Yeah, sure. I'd like that."

"You would?" The sheer joy radiating from Vanessa's dark eyes almost did him in. He was suddenly willing to do anything—stand on his head or turn cartwheels—if it made her this happy.

"Yes." He offered a hesitant smile. "I don't know Pastor Harmon, though. I haven't been to church services since I've been back on base. Between my flashbacks and fighting through the red-tape bureaucracy, I felt completely alone, with the military red tape in getting Beacon home dragging me down." He took a step toward her, silently pleading for her to understand. "But then, I came here in time to prevent the masked man from stealing the puppies. I prayed, desperately and reverently, for your safety and Aiden's. Now that you and Aiden are safe, it makes me think God must have been watching over you.

Over me, too." His voice dropped to a whisper. "I was wrong to stay away for so long."

"I'm so happy to hear you say that." Vanessa smiled tremulously, looking as if she might cry. "It's during times of stress that we need Him the most. And I'm extremely grateful God brought you into my life, Isaac. Not just because of your incredible timing, but because I've never met someone like you. Someone who bravely faces adversity with steely determination."

"Vanessa." Her name came out as a groan. She moved toward him at the same time he reached for her. Then she was in his arms, where she belonged, and he was kissing her the way he'd longed to do from the moment he'd realized she was safe.

"You're so beautiful," he murmured, reveling in her softness.

"You're not so bad, yourself," she whispered, tipping her head back to look up at him.

He stared at her dainty features, as if to memorize the expression of desire on her sweet face and moist lips. Yet at the same time, he knew that this couldn't go anywhere. He forced himself to move backward, putting space between them. "You need to get some sleep. Good night, Vanessa."

"Good night, Isaac." She pulled out of his

arms and moved away, disappearing down the hallway leading to the bedrooms.

He stood where he was for several long moments, telling himself he'd done the right thing. She deserved someone better. Someone whole. Someone with a future.

And none of that applied to him.

He finally stretched out on the sofa, ignoring the blanket but resting his head on the pillow.

Breathing deep, he inwardly groaned. The pillow carried Vanessa's honeysuckle scent.

Tormenting him with what he'd never have.

NINE

The incessant ringing of her phone dragged Vanessa awake, blinking groggily in the sunlight streaming through her window. Squinting against the glare, she fumbled for the phone. "Gomez," she answered in a hoarse voice.

"This is Captain Blackwood. Lieutenant General Hall would like to see you and Captain Goddard at zero nine hundred hours."

"Uh, okay." She pushed her hair behind her ear. "What time is it now?"

"Zero seven thirty. See you then." Justin disconnected the line.

She had just over an hour, which wasn't a lot of time, especially when she was still exhausted from her eventful night. Sleep hadn't come easily, especially after Isaac's toe-curling kiss.

He'd called her beautiful. And unlike Leo, who called everyone gorgeous, she sensed he'd really meant it.

Or maybe that's what she wanted to believe.

Shaking her head at her foolishness, she ducked into the bathroom, showered and then changed into her dress blues. She idly wondered why Isaac's attendance was required, then figured it must be because he had firsthand information about the attack that she didn't.

The formal request had to be related to the early-morning invasion of her home. Why else would the base commander ask to see them?

She walked into the kitchen, surprised to be greeted by the enticing scent of coffee. Isaac stood leaning against the counter, sipping from a mug. He eyed her cautiously over the rim.

"Did you talk to Justin?"

She nodded and helped herself to a cup of the steaming brew. "You, too?"

He nodded. "I didn't want to leave without making sure you were up, but I need to get home to shower and change."

"Understood. Do you want to meet here in thirty minutes?"

He hesitated, then shrugged. "Sure. Half an hour is a lot of time. It won't take us that long."

"I just don't want to be late for a meeting with the top brass." She grimaced. "That would be a CLM for sure."

He lifted a curious brow. "A what?"

"Career Limiting Move."

Isaac chuckled. "Okay, then. Thirty minutes

it is." He downed the last of his coffee and set his mug in the sink. "See you soon."

"Sure." She carried her mug and followed him as he took Tango and left through the front door. Aiden wasn't out there, but was in the backyard, working with the puppies.

Her brother really seemed to have a connection with the animals and she couldn't help wondering once again if it was possible that he could get reassigned to the K-9 training center. She made a mental note to discuss the possibility with Westley James, although she knew it wasn't completely up to him. Aiden was on medical leave and he needed permission from not only his current captain, but Lieutenant Colonel Flintman's recommendation, as well.

"Hi, Aiden," she greeted him, then turned and nodded at the cop stationed outside the door. "How are the national parks doing this morning?"

"You should see how well trained they are," Aiden gushed over the progress the puppies had made. "Even with their mother recuperating at the vet, they're getting the hang of this. They're truly amazing."

"Because of you," she reminded him. "You're doing an awesome job with them. Hey, I have a meeting at Base Command at nine. What time is your doctor's appointment?"

"Um, not sure. Maybe three this afternoon?" Aiden answered distractedly. "Why?"

"You asked me to watch the pups, remember?" She wondered if her brother was suffering from lapses in memory, which was not unheard of in cases of PTSD.

"Oh, yeah. Right. Aw, good girl, Shenandoah, you're managing to keep up with your brothers and sister." Aiden lifted the runt of the litter and snuggled with her for a moment.

She smiled. "I'll make sure I'm back well before fifteen hundred, okay?"

"Uh-huh."

She left him with the pups, and made a quick breakfast. After eating her omelet, she made one for Aiden. She worried about him. He was so focused on the puppies, she wasn't sure he was taking care of himself.

Isaac arrived in exactly thirty minutes as promised and they left for the meeting. She brought Eagle with her, for added protection and so Aiden would have one less animal to worry about. Her loyal and protective K-9 jumped into the back of the SUV without any trouble.

Impeccably handsome in his dress blues, Isaac smiled and nodded as he slid into the passenger seat.

"Where's Tango?"

"I left him at home." Isaac slid into the passenger seat and closed the door. "If there's time, I'd like to stop by the vet on the way back, to check on Beacon."

"Have you heard from Kyle?"

"Not yet." Isaac's expression was troubled. "I'm hoping no news is good news."

"I agree. I'm sure Kyle would let you know if there was a change for the worse."

Isaac nodded, but didn't say anything further. A strained silence filled the car, making her wonder what was going on in Isaac's mind.

She told herself he was probably reviewing the sequence of events from yesterday. The gunfire at the Winged Java, followed by the nightmare and the attempt to steal the puppies, were probably replaying over and over in his head.

Hopefully, he didn't regret their kiss—or worse, agreeing to go to church services with her.

She parked on the street and slid out from behind the wheel, releasing the back so Eagle could jump down. Clipping the leash to Eagle's collar, she walked beside Isaac.

Because they were a few minutes early, they were shown into a small reception area to wait for Captain Blackwood. Eagle sat tall beside her and she scratched the Doberman between the ears.

She'd gotten Eagle a few months ago, when

events had escalated on base. The top brass had agreed that anyone targeted by the Red Rose Killer could keep their K-9s at home with them at all times. The smart Doberman had accepted her without a problem, and she was thrilled to have him as a guard dog.

Ten minutes later, the door opened and Justin beckoned to them. "Lieutenant General Hall is ready for us."

Vanessa felt unaccountably nervous, second-guessing her decision to bring Eagle along for this meeting. She'd wanted to be sure the general knew she was taking the threat seriously, but she wished now she'd left Eagle behind.

She entered the room first, greeting Lieutenant General Nathan Hall with a sharp salute. "First Lieutenant Vanessa Gomez, sir."

Isaac mirrored her salute. "Captain Isaac Goddard, sir."

"At ease," the base commander said after returning their salutes. "Have a seat."

Vanessa sat and gave Eagle the hand signal to sit, too. The dog dropped onto his haunches, sitting tall, ears perked forward as if awaiting his next command.

"I understand there was a break-in at your home early this morning." Lieutenant General Hall steepled his hands together, gazing at them intently. "A civilian wearing a black mask was killed at the scene."

A civilian? She risked a quick glance at Isaac.

"I stumbled upon the masked intruder attempting to steal a box of puppies from Lieutenant Gomez's home," Isaac said. "He threw them at me and pulled a knife. He ran after I disarmed him, so I gave chase. Unfortunately, he attempted to cross the road right in front of a large semitruck delivering supplies, and he was hit and killed on impact."

Base Commander Lieutenant General Hall nodded. "Lieutenant, does the name Ricardo Meyer mean anything to you?"

Vanessa blinked. "No, sir. Is that the identity of the civilian?"

"He apparently worked at the hospital as a janitor," Lieutenant General Hall continued without directly answering her question.

Instantly she thought of Joseph Kramer, the janitor who died of a Tyraxal overdose. Did these two men know each other? Was it possible that Ricardo blamed her for Joseph's death?

"Lieutenant Gomez?"

She snapped her gaze to meet the commander's. "Sir, I don't know a Ricardo Meyer, but I took care of a civilian janitor named Joseph Kramer who died of a drug overdose a couple of days ago."

The commander's eyebrows levered upward. "You think they're connected?"

"Honestly, sir? I don't see how. Even if we assume the two men were friends, why would Ricardo blame me for Joseph's death? And even if he did, why go after the puppies instead of me personally?"

"Lieutenant, we know Boyd sent you a rose, but we can't find a connection between Ricardo Meyer and Sullivan, either. Is there anyone else who may be upset or angry with you?"

"Captain Leo Turner." The name popped out of her mouth before she could stop it. Her cheeks flushed and she avoided Justin's blatantly curious gaze. "I broke off my relationship with the captain several months ago."

"Has he been harassing you?" Justin asked.

She forced herself to meet his gaze, hoping her embarrassment wasn't too obvious. "No, he hasn't. However, he's the only other person I've argued with over the past few months. I don't believe he hired someone to invade my home, but I wanted to be completely honest about who might be upset with me."

"Thank you, Lieutenant, we will take that information under advisement," Lieutenant General Hall said.

"Sir, may I ask whether or not you believe Ricardo Meyer is linked to the Olio Crime Organization?" Isaac asked.

There was a heavy pause before the commander spoke. "We don't have any evidence of that at this time. Captain Goddard, I assume you also don't know Ricardo Meyer?"

"No, sir."

"Well then, thank you for coming in on such short notice." Lieutenant General Hall rose to his feet, so she and Isaac stood, too. "You're dismissed."

They saluted the commander and waited until he left the conference room. Then Justin shrugged his shoulders. "I'll be in touch," he said before following his boss out.

Vanessa released her pent-up breath, glancing down at Eagle, who'd behaved admirably during the meeting. "Doesn't look as if they're going to tell us anything more."

"Guess not," Isaac agreed.

They left Base Command and returned to Vanessa's SUV. She opened the windows to air it out before asking Eagle to jump in the back.

She headed back down Canyon Drive. "Do you want to stop at the veterinary clinic?"

He hesitated, then nodded. "I'm sorry to hear about your relationship."

"Yeah, well, trust me—I'm happy I learned about his cheating before things got too serious."

She glanced at him. "I felt like an idiot when I realized everyone else suspected long before I found out."

"He's a jerk, not worth your time."

"Thanks, I appreciate that."

He shifted uncomfortably in his seat. "I was in a relationship before the crash, but Amber couldn't handle the way I'd changed after the traumatic event." He glanced at her. "I'm not good relationship material."

It was on the tip of her tongue to argue, but then she realized what he was really saying. This was Isaac's way of warning her off. His way of telling her not to expect anything from him, despite their amazing kiss.

Her stomach knotted and she tightened her grip on the steering wheel. She didn't agree with Isaac's assessment. That was something he needed to figure out for himself.

Isaac inwardly grimaced as his statement hung like a radioactive force field between them. He hadn't intended to come across so blunt, but it was probably better in the long run.

He'd spent what had been left of last night wide-awake in a vain attempt to keep Vanessa from invading his dreams. He couldn't ever remember feeling so tied up in knots over a woman.

She pulled over to the curb in front of the veterinary clinic and parked in one of the short-term slots. He almost wished she wasn't coming in with him but he needed to remain with her, refusing to go back on his promise to protect her.

He went around back and stood in front of her, casting a glance up and down the road. "Ready?"

"Of course."

Keeping her and Eagle in front of him, he entered the clinic and caught Airman Fielding's eyes. "Is Captain Roark busy? I'd like to check on Beacon."

"He was examining Beacon earlier. Let me get him for you." The young woman left the main desk, returning in less than a minute. "Captain Roark has Beacon settled in exam room number three."

It was frustrating to have to see Beacon in the exam rooms, but sensed it would be better than touching him through the metal bars of a kennel. He entered the exam room, suddenly feeling an odd sense of peace that Vanessa was beside him.

Kyle stood next to the table, holding Beacon's collar. The German shepherd lifted his head and thumped his tail as Isaac approached. "Hey, buddy. You're looking better today." He bent over to bury his face in Beacon's neck.

"He is better today," Kyle confirmed. "The

area of hemorrhage has shrunk considerably, which is a good sign."

The news was a balm of relief. "I'm glad to hear it."

Kyle stroked Beacon's fur. "He was definitely feisty last night, giving Airman Fielding a hard time."

"I'd apologize except that's Beacon's normal nature, which makes me happy," Isaac said with a wry smile. "It must mean he's getting better."

"I think so, too." Kyle gave a nod of satisfaction. "In fact, if the CT scan looks good tomorrow, I'm inclined to send him home with you."

"I'd love it," Isaac said. "As long as you think he'll be okay."

"I wouldn't discharge him if I wasn't sure of that." Kyle stepped back. "I'll give you a few minutes, then I need to get him back to the kennel."

Isaac murmured reassurances to the animal, much the way he had when they were stranded on the edge of a mountainside. Vanessa didn't say anything, but having her there was more than enough.

"Ready to go?" he asked her a few moments later, breaking the silence.

"Sure," Vanessa agreed.

As they walked outside to where Vanessa had left her SUV, he noticed a brunette walking beside a medium-size Belgian Malinois. There was something familiar about her facial features…

Then it hit him. She was Jacey Burke, Jake's younger sister. He remembered Jake telling him how they'd both joined the Air Force out of high school and had both become dog handlers.

Jake's lifeless eyes flashed in his memory, accompanied by a flash of panic. He shoved the image away with an effort.

By the time he'd gotten himself under control, Jacey was within arm's reach. He reminded himself that this was his best friend's sister and that she deserved his respect and support.

"Hi, Jacey." He forced a smile.

"Captain Goddard," Jacey greeted him with a salute, including Vanessa in that. "Greta, sit."

The Malinois sat.

He returned the professional courtesy with a salute, then waved a hand. "No need to be formal, and please, call me Isaac. And this is First Lieutenant Vanessa Gomez."

Her smile was sad, but she nodded. "How are you?"

"I'm good." Early in the process of getting Beacon home, he'd called Jacey and asked if she minded his taking her brother's dog and she'd gladly approved. "Beacon is here on base, but there was a small accident, so he's being watched by the vet for a few days."

"Oh, I hope he's okay." Her brow furrowed with concern.

"He will be," he assured her. "I'm surprised to see you here, though. I'd heard you were overseas."

Her deep blue eyes, so much like Jake's, were shadowed with grief. "I returned from my tour in Afghanistan two weeks ago," she informed him. "Greta and I have been assigned to the training center for the foreseeable future."

"Really? I'm glad to hear it," he said. "Master Sergeant Westley James could use the help."

"That's what I've been told," Jacey agreed. Her expression remained troubled. "It's nice to be stateside for a while."

The way she avoided his direct gaze bothered him. He'd always been able to tell when something was bugging Jake, too. "Are you okay?"

"Of course." Her smile didn't reach her eyes. "Greta is scheduled for a checkup, so I figured I'd take her myself." She hesitated, shrugged. "She had a rough tour."

Isaac understood that meant Jacey had likely suffered a rough tour, as well. Dog handlers did everything with their K-9 partners.

"If you need something, let me know." He glanced at Vanessa, who hadn't said anything during the brief meeting.

"I will." Again, she avoided his direct gaze. "Nice to see you, Isaac. Lieutenant Gomez."

"It was nice meeting you," Vanessa agreed.

"Good day, Captain." Jacey gave him a quick nod, then gave Greta a hand signal that brought the beautiful animal to her feet.

Jacey walked around them and disappeared inside the veterinary clinic.

"She looks upset," Vanessa said.

"Yeah." Isaac gazed after her, sick with the realization that Jacey blamed him for her brother's death. Six months ago, when he'd called about Beacon, she'd sounded friendly enough, but her reaction face-to-face proved otherwise.

And he couldn't blame her.

If only he'd reacted quicker, had found a spot to land the damaged chopper sooner. Maybe Jake and his copilot would have survived.

Her brother's death was his fault. And how ironic that Jake's K-9 partner, Beacon, had been the one to save his life.

TEN

After dropping a silently brooding Isaac off at home, Vanessa battled a deep sense of loss that weighed heavily across her shoulders as she parked the SUV in her driveway and let Eagle out. Justin had arranged for additional protection after the shooting incident at the Winged Java, so she wasn't surprised to see a cop at the door. He saluted, and she returned the acknowledgment. She waited for the Doberman to do his business before taking him inside.

She gave Eagle food and water, glad Aiden was preoccupied with feeding the puppies in the bathtub. The last thing her brother needed was to notice the lingering hint of despair in her eyes.

She told herself it was ridiculous to be this upset over a man who'd kissed her. Leo's cheating on her was a much bigger betrayal. Although to be honest, Isaac's withdrawal hurt worse than Leo's cheating.

Was that messed up, or what?

She gave herself a mental shake. She wasn't interested in a relationship, so why did it matter? Still, the rest of the day loomed empty before her, and it struck her just how much time she'd spent with Isaac over the past few days.

If she wasn't needed to watch the puppies this afternoon during Aiden's therapy appointment, she would have called the hospital and offered to work a partial shift to help keep her hands and mind busy.

She blew out a heavy breath. Okay, since heading to the hospital was out of the question for now, maybe she should work with Eagle a bit more, refreshing the training the handlers had walked through with her a few months ago.

Outside, she put Eagle through the paces, pleased with his response. When her cell phone rang, her heart leaped.

Isaac?

No. Recognizing the number as from within the hospital, she grimaced and answered, "Lieutenant Gomez."

"This is Lieutenant Colonel Flintman. I apologize for my delay in returning your call."

"Lieutenant Colonel Flintman, I'm so happy to hear from you." Finally, the doctor had called her back.

"I'm sorry to hear about these drug overdoses," he said in a concerned tone. "It's horrible to learn Tyraxal is being abused like this."

"I agree, sir. Three overdoses are three too many."

"Lieutenant Gomez, I'm proud of how you identified this issue and raised the alarm," he said warmly. "Nice job. Do you remember the patients' names? I need to file a report about these adverse drug reactions with the Food and Drug Administration. The FDA tracks this sort of thing very closely."

She was relieved to hear Lieutenant Colonel Flintman was taking her concerns seriously. She readily gave him the three names, each patient's face burned into her memory. She could hear him clattering on a keyboard.

"Lieutenant Colonel Flintman, what do you think of the fact that Joseph Kramer was a civilian working as a janitor at the hospital?"

"I find it very disturbing," he replied. "I can only assume that one of the airmen I'm treating has decided to sell his or her prescription."

"Yes, that's the same conclusion I came to, as well." Vanessa thought again of her brother, secretly relieved he wasn't taking Tyraxal. He was doing so much better now that he'd been caring for the puppies, she hoped he wouldn't need the medication moving forward, either. She silently thanked God for watching over him. "I'm glad you're planning to report this to the FDA. I think the addictive effect of Tyraxal clearly outweighs the benefit."

"Well, now, I don't know if I'd go that far," Lieutenant Colonel Flintman said, a hint of steel in his tone. "You know as well as I do, Lieutenant, that each patient responds differently to medications. Some of my patients have found Tyraxal very beneficial. Unfortunately, like many medications, they don't each help everyone in the same way."

"You're right," she agreed, properly chastised. Flintman had a good point; she knew firsthand that every patient responded differently to medications and treatments. It happened in the critical care setting all the time. "Let's hope that we don't see any more overdoses."

"Agreed."

"Thank you again, sir, for returning my call."

"Of course, Lieutenant. After all, it's nurses like you that are the key to our hospital's success."

"Thank you, sir."

There was a pause before the psychiatrist spoke again. "Lieutenant Gomez, I don't want to overstep my bounds here, but may I ask how your brother is doing?"

She was surprised by his question. "He's doing great, sir."

"Good, good." He coughed, then continued, "I must say, I'm a little concerned because Aiden has canceled his last two therapy appointments, including the one we had scheduled for this afternoon. He claims he's far too busy taking care of a litter of puppies to come in to see me."

Vanessa was shocked by the news of the canceled appointments. "I had no idea," she managed.

"It's good he has something like the puppies to help him through this," Lieutenant Colonel Flintman continued. "But you know as well as I do how important therapy is. After all this great progress, I'd hate to see him suffer a relapse."

She didn't want that, either. "I'll talk to him, sir."

"Thank you, Lieutenant."

She disconnected the call and, summoning Eagle, headed inside. Her timing was good, because Aiden was emerging from the bathroom, carrying the box of puppies.

"Hey," he greeted her with a broad smile. "I didn't realize you were back."

"I was working with Eagle outside." She tried to think of a way to broach the subject of Aiden's missed appointments. "How are the puppies doing today?"

"They're amazing." Aiden's voice was full of

pride. "I can't believe how far they've come over these past few days."

She nodded, thrilled at how her brother had taken the task of fostering them so seriously. "I'm caring for them this afternoon, right? I think you mentioned having a therapy appointment."

Aiden's smile faded and his gaze skittered from hers. "No need. I rescheduled that."

"Rescheduled? Or canceled?"

"What difference does it make?" Aiden asked, bristling. "I'm doing fine."

"You're doing incredibly well," she acknowledged, stepping toward him. "And I'm truly thrilled about your progress. But, Aiden, ongoing treatment is important. I'm asking you to please, please reschedule your appointment. Don't keep skipping them entirely."

Aiden shifted the box in his grasp and edged around her. "I'll think about it."

She didn't want to let him go without a firm commitment. "I've heard the doc is taking appointments on Saturday," she pressed. "I'm working tomorrow, but I'm sure Isaac would watch the puppies for an hour or so. And if that doesn't work for some reason, I'm off Monday."

Aiden didn't answer for a long moment. "Okay," he finally agreed. "I'll call and schedule for Monday."

She drew in a deep breath and let it out slowly. She would have preferred Saturday, but wasn't going to argue. "Thank you," she murmured. "I hope you realize I only want you to get better."

"I know, Nessa." Aiden flashed a crooked smile. "Speaking of helping me, how about lending a hand with the next bout of housebreaking?"

"Do I have to?" she asked with a mock grimace. "That's not exactly my favorite job."

"Mine, either. But it's still rewarding when they get it right."

She chuckled in agreement. "I'm in."

The afternoon passed pleasantly enough, but she could feel her stomach knot with tension as evening approached. She'd committed to attending a homecoming party for some returning airmen, promising her best friend, Margie Campbell, that she'd come. But she knew now she needed to cancel. It wasn't worth the risk. There had been too many attempts to kill her.

She found herself growing angry with Boyd Sullivan. She'd helped him that night all those years ago and this was how he repaid her? By trying to strangle her? Shoot at her not just once, but twice? Convince people to do dirty deeds on his behalf, like trying to steal the puppies?

From the very beginning, Boyd has demonstrated weird and erratic behavior.

The worst part of it all was not knowing what he'd do next.

Isaac tried to forget about the pain and sadness in Jacey Burke's eyes and to focus on what was going right instead. Kyle had reassured him that Beacon was doing much better and may be released as early as the following morning.

After picking up lunch at Carmen's, he headed home. For some reason, the food didn't taste quite as good as it had when he'd eaten it with Vanessa and Aiden.

As if sensing his mood, Tango came over and rested his head in Isaac's lap. He smiled and scratched Tango behind the ears. The golden had been a reliable companion for him over the past few months, while he'd dealt with the red tape of getting Beacon returned home. And now that his time with Tango was coming to an end, he knew he'd miss the dog's calming presence.

Maybe he should head over to see if Aiden was interested in taking Tango as a therapy dog. The kid deserved a second chance, and he'd appeared to enjoy the golden.

He was halfway to the front door when he abruptly stopped. Who was he kidding? This wasn't about Aiden at all. No, this was nothing more than a pathetic excuse to see Vanessa.

Idiot.

He belatedly remembered there was an airmen's homecoming party scheduled for early evening. Was Vanessa planning to go? He didn't know, but after everything that had happened recently, he thought not.

Which was too bad, because he wanted to go with her. Very much. Even though he shouldn't.

He dropped onto the sofa and buried his head in his hands. This emotional Cuban Eight aerobatic maneuver his brain was doing was driving him crazy. What was wrong with him that he wanted what he couldn't have?

The reasons he needed to stay away from Vanessa were murky at best, like flying through a thick storm cloud with zero visibility.

Vanessa wasn't Amber, so why was he constantly comparing the two?

Because he was afraid the end result would be the same.

And why wouldn't it be? He still didn't know what his future held. If he couldn't be a pilot because of his PTSD, then what sort of job could he do?

There was no denying the possibility that his future may not include remaining in the Air Force.

With abrupt determination, he surged to his feet and pulled out his phone. He dialed Justin, hoping his former Air Force Academy buddy wasn't still tied up in meetings at Base Command.

"Blackwood."

"Hey, Justin. I'm sorry to bother you, but do you have a minute?"

"Yeah, my next meeting isn't for a half hour. What's going on?"

"This isn't about Boyd," he reassured Justin. "It's personal."

"Related to a beautiful petite brunette?" Justin teased.

"No, I'm looking for some career advice." He didn't bother to add that part of the driving force behind the sudden phone call was, in fact, Vanessa. "I'm due to reenlist and I'd like to discuss possible career options."

"Of course," Justin agreed. "Oops, there goes my phone. Listen, it's a little crazy right now with all this stuff going on, but I promise we'll find some time to talk, okay?"

"Great, thanks." Isaac felt better for having broached the touchy subject that had been secretly weighing him down for months now. "I appreciate your time."

"We'll set something up soon," Justin promised.

Isaac disconnected from the call. "One step at a time," he said to Tango.

The golden thumped his tail on the floor.

Sitting around at home was driving him crazy. Was Vanessa feeling the same way? He remembered how she'd bristled at the thought of being confined to her house. Going to the airmen's homecoming party might be a welcome distraction. Not as a date, but as a way to get out of the house for a while.

Once the idea took hold in his mind, he couldn't shake it loose. He was going to do it. Within a couple of hours, he was showered, shaved and changed into a fresh set of dress blues. With Tango on a leash at his side, he left his house a good thirty minutes before the party to walk over to Vanessa's. He didn't have her number, so he would have to ask her face-to-face.

His pulse kicked up a notch with anticipation, as if it had been days rather than hours since he'd seen her last.

Yep, he had it bad.

He strode up to the front door, returning the cop's salute. "Is Lieutenant Gomez inside?"

"Um, yes, sir." The cop moved over, allowing him to enter.

"Isaac." Vanessa's expression indicated surprise when she saw him walk in. "What are you doing here?"

"I thought you'd be going a little crazy sitting around, and you might want to get out of here for a while. We could stop in at the airfield and watch the homecoming."

Her eyes flashed with anticipation, but then she frowned. "I would, but it's too dangerous."

"We won't stay long." He didn't understand why he was suddenly so desperate to go with her. "You deserve to have a little fun, don't you?"

"I don't know…" Her voice trailed off. Then she shrugged. "Okay, why not? Give me a few minutes to change."

"Happy to wait." He hoped his relief wasn't too obvious. He really needed to pull himself together.

Ten minutes later, she returned in her dress blues. "I'll drive."

He didn't argue, but followed her out to the SUV in the driveway. He didn't see anyone around, but the sense of being watched had returned. His PTSD paranoia? Or true danger?

They made it to the landing strip with time to spare. As they made their way through the crowd, he noticed a tall blonde waving at them.

"Hey, Margie," Vanessa called. "How are you?"

"Great." Margie glanced at him, so he stepped forward.

"Captain Isaac Goddard," he said, introducing himself.

"First Lieutenant Margie Campbell," the blonde returned. "Vanessa and I work together. Nice to meet you, Captain," Margie said with a smile. She turned toward Vanessa. "I'm supposed to meet Tristen here. Have you seen him?"

"Not yet. But you can hang with us for a while," Vanessa offered.

"Oh, I don't want to intrude." Margie glanced around, then stood up on her tiptoes. "I think I see Tristen over there. See you later, okay?"

"Sure thing." Vanessa looked a little embarrassed when her friend left. "Don't let Margie make you uncomfortable. She's a ridiculous matchmaker."

Isaac cleared his throat, feeling awkward. "I'm never uncomfortable around you, Vanessa. Quite the opposite."

"Oh." She blushed and looked away.

"I would have called to formally invite you to attend this with me, but didn't have your number."

She arched a brow. "Why would you want it? After all, you're the one who told me you weren't relationship material."

"I'm not," he agreed. "You know, more than anyone else, how I've been struggling since returning stateside."

Her dark gaze filled with compassion. "Oh,

Isaac, struggling with an illness doesn't prevent you from having a relationship."

"It does," he insisted. "Especially when I have more questions than answers about my future."

Understanding dawned in her eyes. "I see. Okay, then why did you change your mind and ask me to come?"

He hesitated, shrugged. "I couldn't stay away."

She muttered something that sounded like *men* under her breath, then wrapped her arm around his waist in a brief hug. He returned the embrace, enjoying the sweet, calming honeysuckle scent that clung to her.

Someone jostled them from behind, forcing him to release her. He lightly grasped her hand, cherishing the connection. "I can't believe how many people showed up for this."

"I know. Any reason to celebrate, right?"

"You got it."

"There's the plane," someone shouted.

Isaac lifted his gaze to the sky, momentarily overwhelmed with a sense of loss. Would he ever make it back up in the pilot's seat? Or was he doomed to be grounded forever?

The C-130 Hercules aircraft slowly grew larger as it approached the runway. The sound of the dual engines was incredibly loud, but that didn't keep him from smiling with appreciation as the pilot leveled the plane, bringing the air-craft in for a smooth landing.

"Nice," he said.

"If you say so." Vanessa shrugged. "I wouldn't know a good landing from a bad one."

"Trust me, you would if you were a passenger inside," he joked.

The plane taxied in toward the hangar. The crowd waited patiently for the plane to stop and for the returning airmen to disembark.

The crowd surrounding them seemed to be holding its collective breath. The C-130 came to a stop and the hatch opened up, dropping to the ground with a loud clang.

After another long moment, the five return-ing airmen appeared from within the depths of the plane, waving as they descended.

"Hey! There's Boyd Sullivan!"

Just like when Beacon arrived on base, chaos erupted. Some people screamed, others pushed and shoved as if attempting to escape, while oth-ers dropped to the ground as if afraid of impend-ing gunfire.

"Stay down," Isaac commanded, pulling Van-essa close. He thought for sure this was nothing more than a ruse to get at Vanessa.

"No! Look. I think I see him over there!" Van-essa pulled away from him and took off running in the direction from where the shout had come from.

"Wait! Vanessa!" Isaac kept pace with her, weaving through people with Tango close to his side. He desperately searched the male faces for Sullivan's familiar features.

Vanessa slowed and stopped, looking around in confusion. "He was here, Isaac. But now he's gone."

"Are you sure?"

"I think so." A hint of doubt invaded her tone.

"Let's join the search." He kept close to her side as they joined other Security Forces officers combing the area for a sign of the Red Rose Killer.

But after frantic searching, they came up empty-handed.

If Boyd Sullivan had in fact been there, he was gone now.

Evading capture once again.

ELEVEN

Hours later, after fruitless searching, they were gathered at Base Command. "Are you absolutely sure you saw Sullivan?" Captain Blackwood was frowning at Vanessa as if she'd personally allowed Boyd to escape.

She glanced around the group seated around the table. Several of the members of the task force assigned to catching the Red Rose Killer were in attendance, including Tech Sergeant Linc Colson, First Lieutenant Ethan Webb and Master Sergeant Westley James, none of whom appeared antagonistic, but Yvette Crenville, the base nutritionist, was staring at her suspiciously.

Because Yvette still believed she was guilty of the false claims the anonymous blogger had made about her helping Boyd?

Or because Yvette had noticed Vanessa keeping a close eye on her recently? Justin Blackwood had asked her to watch Yvette while they were both at work, so she had. But the woman had yet to do anything the least bit suspicious.

"No, I can't be absolutely sure I saw him." Vanessa tried to keep her impatience from showing. "Everyone heard the shout and when I looked in that direction, I caught a glimpse of dark hair and narrow eyes. In that brief moment, I thought the man was Boyd."

"Anyone else see him?" Justin asked.

A strained silence fell over the group and those around her all shook their heads.

"We may not have, but someone did," Isaac pointed out. "Someone shouted his name, causing instant pandemonium."

Vanessa wished she'd kept the flash of recognition to herself. The glimpse had been so fleeting, and looking back, she could admit the dark-haired, narrow-eyed man could have been anyone.

Justin blew out a frustrated breath. "Great. This is just perfect. What I'm hearing is that we don't know if Sullivan was really there or not," he said. "In fact, it's highly likely the person who shouted Sullivan's name saw the same guy Vanessa spotted."

Once again, all eyes turned toward her. She really, really wished she'd kept her mouth shut. "But haven't there been other sightings of Boyd on base? Why is it so hard to believe he was in the crowd this evening?"

"Because if he was smart, he'd stay hidden," Westley James said. "And while Boyd may not be the most brilliant criminal we've come across, he's had us chasing our tails for months now. We've seriously underestimated him."

She couldn't argue with the master sergeant. "But if Boyd is on base, then there must be a methodical way to find him. Have we gone through all the videos and checked out every possible person who might be helping him? I promise it's not me." Her voice came out more vehemently than she intended.

"No one suspects you, Vanessa," Isaac said. "You were attacked at the hospital and have the bruises to prove it, not to mention being shot at several times."

While she appreciated Isaac's support, the collar of her dress uniform hid the bruises from view. Justin had seen her bruises that first night, but no one else had. And so far, no one could prove that the gunshots had been directed at her.

Deep down, she could understand some of the skepticism. Being targeted by Boyd didn't make any sense. She'd helped him that night in the alley all those years ago. There was no reason for him to come after her now.

"Now that you mention other helpers, I have

noticed something odd," Gretchen Hill said. Vanessa was relieved when all eyes turned toward the female cop.

"Like what?" Justin demanded.

Gretchen tipped her chin and met Justin's direct gaze. "One night I worked late with our newest dog, Abby. After returning her to the kennel, I found one of the trainers, a guy named Rusty Morton, acting very strangely. He was pacing and texting, looking worried. The night was cool but he was sweating and appeared nervous. When he saw me, he tucked his phone away and left the training facility." Gretchen shrugged. "I thought it was odd."

Justin's gaze was skeptical, but then Westley James nodded. "You know, I've noticed him acting weird, too. I found him sitting outside the other day, his head in his hands as if he didn't know what to do. I asked if he was okay, and he admitted he wasn't feeling well, told me he'd caught a bug of some kind. Then he hurried away."

Justin looked thoughtful. "It's strange behavior, but have you considered the possibility that he was just trying to hide his illness?"

"Why would he hide something like that?" Gretchen asked.

"As a nurse, I know many people don't like admitting they're sick," Vanessa said slowly.

"And one conclusion could be that he's afraid Westley will take away his position as a trainer. But all of that aside, I don't think we can ignore the possibility that Morton might be helping Boyd. After all, someone let all the dogs out of their kennels as a diversion."

There was a long moment of silence.

"Rusty loves those dogs," Westley said. "But I've had the same concern."

Justin swept his gaze over the room. "Since we don't have any other leads, I'll assign a cop to keep an eye on Morton for the next few days." Justin paused, then asked, "Anything else going on that I should know about?"

More silence, then a round of *no sirs* echoed from the group.

"Good. Dismissed." Justin rose to his feet.

Vanessa happened to be seated closest to the door, so she gratefully slipped out ahead of the group.

"Vanessa, wait!" Isaac's voice rose above the din of departing airmen.

She slowed down enough to let Isaac catch up, but continued making her way outside the building, breathing the fresh autumn air.

"Vanessa, you can't go off on your own." Isaac's voice was tense with alarm.

"I know, I'm sorry."

He stood beside her for a moment, Tango at

his side. She greeted the dog with a quick rub, glad to see him, considering she'd left Eagle at home.

But hearing Boyd's name and the subsequent chaos had made her wish she'd brought her protective K-9 along.

"What's wrong? You seem upset." Isaac's gaze searched hers intently.

She sighed. "It's difficult feeling like I have to constantly profess my innocence."

"You're not a suspect," Isaac assured her.

"I am," she insisted. "And being the only one who claims to have seen Boyd at the landing strip doesn't help my case. I know Justin has told me I'm not a suspect, but that's just words. I won't feel truly vindicated until Boyd is caught and arrested."

"You may be right to some extent," Isaac agreed. "But I know you're innocent."

She was touched by his show of trust. "Thank you."

"Let's walk back to your car."

She nodded and he fell into step beside her, keeping Tango between them. He grimaced. "I should have made you bring Eagle along."

"I know, but after the scare with the intruder, I didn't feel right leaving Aiden home alone with the puppies."

"Justin still has a cop posted at your door," Isaac said.

"Yes, but that didn't help last time, did it?"

"No."

"Exactly." Vanessa shrugged. "I figured being with you would be enough and that Eagle was needed more at home."

"Boyd sent that rose to you, Vanessa. Not to your brother."

She knew that, but the break-in had shaken her confidence. No way was she going to allow Aiden to be hurt because of her.

"You really think Rusty Morton might be involved?" she asked.

"His behavior is off. Could be he's in some kind of trouble," Isaac said. "Makes sense to me that it could be Boyd."

"Maybe he is guilty of something. If he was the one who let the dogs loose, maybe that was only the start and now Boyd is holding that over his head."

"Justin will keep an eye on Rusty. If the trainer is guilty, we'll find out soon enough."

They walked for a while in silence and she wondered if Isaac had put Tango between them on purpose, to keep space between them. But if he wanted distance, why had he showed up at her doorstep to take her to the homecoming? It confused her.

When they reached her SUV, they exchanged mobile phone numbers.

"Does this mean that you're still attending church services with me and Aiden on Sunday?"

She didn't imagine the slight hesitation before he said, "Yes, of course."

There was no *of course* about it, but she didn't push. Just because Isaac wasn't interested in a relationship, she still wanted him to find a way back to his faith.

Believing in God and leaning on His grace and wisdom was important. Far more precious than anything else.

They were both silent on the ride back to her place. He walked with her up to the sidewalk, then stopped. She glanced over her shoulder questioningly.

"I'd like to spend the night on your sofa."

"That's not necessary," she said with a nod to the cop at the door. "I'm sure we'll be fine. Besides, I have to work a twelve-hour shift tomorrow, so I'll be up super early."

"Please." Isaac took a step closer. "Humor me. I promised to keep you safe and after the possible sighting of Boyd, I can't stand the thought of leaving you."

"If it makes you feel better, why not?" She saluted the cop at the door, then went inside, Isaac and Tango right behind her.

Aiden was sitting on the kitchen floor, surrounded by the puppies. "Hi. How was the party?"

"Nothing special." Vanessa didn't want her brother to worry about Boyd. "Isaac is going to bunk on the sofa if that's okay with you."

"Sure. I'll keep the puppies in my room tonight." Aiden's expression turned grim. "I'm not going to risk letting anything happen to them."

"Good idea." Vanessa couldn't help but smile when Tango went over to sniff the pups, making Aiden laugh.

It had been so long since her brother had laughed.

She stood awkwardly for a moment, secretly wishing for an opportunity to be alone with Isaac. But it was probably better to give Aiden and Isaac some time alone, in case they wanted to talk. "Well, good night, then. Don't forget, I'm working a full twelve tomorrow."

"I know." Her brother's voice held a note of annoyance. She needed to remember that despite everything he'd gone through, he wasn't a little kid anymore. At twenty, he was far from the boy she'd helped raise with their aunt Millie after their parents had died.

She left the two men alone, hoping and praying that Aiden was truly on the road to recovery.

* * *

Isaac wasn't sure why he was torturing himself by sleeping on Vanessa's sofa, surrounding himself with her honeysuckle scent. Wasn't one night of no sleep enough?

Or maybe he was hoping that he wouldn't suffer another nightmare if he was here at her place, rather than alone in his house.

He made a mental note to seek out Jacey Burke again to at least apologize for his role in her brother's death. If she couldn't forgive him, that was fine, but he at least needed to let her know he held himself responsible.

The way any good pilot would.

He sat with Aiden for a while. They didn't talk about their respective nightmares, but he sensed the young man was beginning to trust him. Maybe over time, Aiden would feel comfortable opening up to Isaac.

Ironic that the only person he'd opened up to was Vanessa.

Eventually, Isaac slept better than he'd hoped. When he woke, it was to the tantalizing scent of coffee. He pried open one eye and peered into the kitchen.

Vanessa looked lovely, her golden skin glowing from her shower, her dark hair pulled away from her face in a ponytail that made her look years younger. His heart stumbled in his chest and he had to force himself to stay where he was or risk kissing her again.

"Hey," he said, drawing her attention. "Let me know when you're ready to go. I'll walk with you to work."

"I have about five minutes, but that's not enough time to walk, so I'll drive." She finished her cup of coffee and then set it in the sink. "Actually, now that I think about it, maybe you should drive me to work? That way I can keep Eagle here with Aiden."

"You need Eagle more than Aiden does." He shot to his feet.

"He can't stay in the ICU all day and besides, Aiden needs protection, too."

He recognized the stubborn glint in her eyes. "Please?"

"Not happening." She narrowed her gaze and thrust out her chin. "Will you drive with me or not?"

"Okay." He sensed arguing wasn't going to get him anywhere and felt a twinge of resentment that she was pushing the issue of driving after he'd already told her about his concern of triggering a flashback. "But I'm going to leave your car at the hospital. Kyle is going to release Beacon today, so I'll hang around the Winged Java for a while until the clinic opens."

"Okay." She picked up her purse and her stethoscope. "Let's go."

"Will you stop in and check on Aiden later today?" she asked as she glanced at him. "I'd feel better knowing he has someone around while I'm working."

"I can do that." He cleared his throat and cast a look at Tango in the rear. "Maybe I'll leave Tango, see if he'll bond with him."

"That's great. And I'm really happy to hear about Beacon coming home, too. You've certainly waited long enough for this day."

"You have that right." Isaac still had trouble believing it for himself. "Park close to the door, okay? And call me after your shift so I can come meet you."

She nodded, and obliged him by pulling into the first available space close to the building. He slid out of the passenger seat as she emerged with her purse over her shoulder and her stethoscope slung around her neck. He escorted her to the door.

"Have a great day." He gave her a quick hug, releasing her before he could act on his temptation to kiss her. "See you later."

"Bye."

He stood on the sidewalk, watching as she hurried inside. When the door closed behind her, he led Tango toward the Winged Java.

After purchasing a coffee and blueberry muffin, he headed back outside to one of the tables along the sidewalk.

The clinic didn't open for over two hours yet, so when he finished his muffin, he settled in for a long wait.

A familiar female figure approached on the sidewalk, dressed casually in her battle-ready uniform. He recognized Greta, her Belgian Malinois, walking at her side.

"Jacey?" He quickly stood. "Hey, do you have a minute?"

"Oh, hi, Isaac." Her smile was strained. "Um, sure, I guess."

"I won't keep you long," he promised. Now that she was here, he tried to formulate the best approach. "Do you want coffee or tea?"

"No, thanks." She sat stiffly in the seat across from him, glancing warily over her shoulder. He frowned, wondering what she'd been through in Afghanistan.

"Listen, Jacey, I just wanted a chance to apologize to you." Isaac swallowed hard and forced himself to meet her startled gaze. "I know it's my fault your brother is gone and I feel terrible for letting you down."

"You were under attack by enemy fire," she said. "I don't hold you responsible for Jake's death. We signed up to serve our country and that's exactly what you and Jake were doing."

He stared in shock. "I—I thought you hated me."

For the first time, her smile brightened her entire face. "I don't hate you, Isaac. Never have." She tipped her head to the side. "Are we okay now?"

"I— Um, yeah, sure." He was flabbergasted at her response. "I'm glad to hear it."

"Are you picking up Beacon today?"

He nodded and finished off his coffee. "Yes, but the clinic doesn't open for a while yet." He grinned. "Somehow, I don't think Kyle will be surprised to find me waiting at the doorway."

She laughed and shook her head. "Probably not." Her smile faded and she glanced again over her shoulder. "Well, I'd better get going. I have some work to do with Greta here."

Isaac's instincts were spinning. "Hey, Jacey, is something wrong? Someone giving you trouble?"

"What?" A flash of guilt shadowed her blue eyes. "Oh, no. I'm fine, truly. Just adapting to life back on US soil, that's all."

He knew what it was like to go from one world where you feared for your life on a daily basis to one where most of the people around you weren't dangerous at all.

Well, except for Boyd Sullivan.

"Jacey, I know Jake would want me to take over the role of big brother to look after you," he said. "Call me if you need something, okay?"

"I will." She bobbed her head in agreement, but he wasn't convinced. "See you later."

The two hours slipped by slowly. Thankfully Kyle Roark arrived ahead of schedule and readily took Isaac back to see Beacon.

The dog lifted his head and let out a sharp bark from his kennel. Then his tail began to wag and his entire body shimmied with excitement.

"He'll be fine, Isaac." Kyle opened the kennel and handed Isaac the leash. He clipped the tether to Beacon's collar and then knelt down to greet the dog the way he'd been wanting to since they'd parted.

"Good boy," he said, chuckling as the dog tried to climb into his lap and lick his face. He rubbed Beacon's coat and buried his face against the dog's neck. "Welcome home, buddy. Welcome home."

Kyle watched the reunion with satisfaction. "It's obvious you two belong together."

"I agree." Isaac finally rose to his feet. "Come on, Beacon. Let's get you home."

Beacon didn't seem to mind Tango, which was a little surprising, since Beacon wasn't what anyone would call a warm and fuzzy animal. He was a warrior.

A warrior that had saved his life.

The morning went by fast, so he didn't make it over to Vanessa's to check on Aiden until after lunch.

"You really want me to watch Tango for a while?" Aiden seemed unsure when Isaac told him his plan. "He's your therapy dog, isn't he?"

"He was, but I have Beacon now. We're a team, and I'm worried that Tango will feel left out."

He spent some of the afternoon getting reacquainted with Beacon, though their connection was so strong, he didn't need the extra time. So he decided to head back to Vanessa's to see how Aiden was doing with Tango.

In no time it was nineteen thirty, the time Vanessa's shift ended. She'd warned him that sometimes she had to work late, but he thought about heading over to meet her, even though she hadn't called yet to say she was finished.

Before he could decide, his phone rang. He grinned when he recognized her number. "Hey, Vanessa."

"Isaac? Someone smashed my driver's-side window and left a red rose on my seat."

TWELVE

Vanessa rubbed her arms, feeling chilled to the bone as she stood beside the cop who'd escorted her to her vehicle. The Security Forces cop had introduced himself as Staff Sergeant Sean Morris and had been happy to provide an escort to her car.

She should have called Isaac, the way they'd initially planned. But she'd thought she'd be safe enough with a cop escort.

And now, she was glad she hadn't been alone when she'd found the damage and the crushed red rose. The implied threat was all too real. Sean Morris had instantly called his boss, while she'd contacted Isaac.

Just hearing Isaac's calm voice had reassured her.

"Captain Blackwood will be here any minute, Lieutenant," Morris said, his blue eyes full of concern. "Are you sure you're okay?"

"Of course," she replied, wishing she could stop shivering. "Frankly, I'm glad it's only my SUV that's been damaged."

Morris didn't look convinced, but he didn't say anything more as twin headlights cut through the darkness. She tensed, until she realized the driver was Justin. He got out of the car and then let his dog, Quinn, out before coming over.

"Captain," Morris greeted the officer with a sharp salute.

"At ease, Sergeant." Justin returned the salute, then his gaze sought hers. "You're not hurt?"

"Sergeant Morris escorted me outside after work and we found this." She gestured to the broken driver's-side window. "Unfortunately, I worked a twelve-hour shift, so I have no idea when this happened."

Justin surveyed the damage, looking grim. "It's a threat all right. Seems to fit in with the way he initially picks his victims, sending a rose then following up with violence. But why is he repeating that pattern now?"

Vanessa battled a helpless wave of anger. "I don't know. None of it makes any sense. He's done so many things, from stealing uniforms, killing people, letting the dogs loose, firing into crowds and leaving threatening notes in all sorts of random places. But the biggest mystery is why he's targeting me in the first place."

"He obviously is carrying a grudge against you," Justin said. "Are you sure you don't know why?"

"No clue." She sighed, then glanced over as Isaac jogged over with Beacon at his side.

He surprised her by pulling her into his arms. "Are you sure you're all right?" he asked in a low, husky voice.

His clean, masculine scent was incredibly soothing. "Yes," she whispered. Oddly enough, now that Isaac was here, she felt much better.

Safer. Which was crazy, since Sergeant Morris was armed and Isaac wasn't.

Isaac held her for another long moment, before releasing his hold so he could examine the damage to her car. "This ridiculousness has gone on long enough," he muttered.

"You don't have to tell me." Justin's tone was laced with frustration. "I hate the way we always seem to be one step behind him."

"We need to check the video cameras, sir," Sergeant Morris said.

"We will, but they haven't helped us so far," Blackwood pointed out. "Sullivan apparently knows where the cameras are and is always wearing a mask or hoodie, keeping his face averted from view. He's managed to avoid motion sensors and other security measures we have, as well."

"Then this fits with Sullivan's previous attempts." Vanessa waved a hand at her broken window.

"Yes, it does," Justin admitted. "Although again, I don't see why he's repeating the pattern, going from attempted murder back to a scare tactic like a brick through a window and a red rose."

"Like the phone call," Vanessa said.

"Phone call?" Blackwood echoed.

She inwardly winced when she realized she'd failed to mention it. "I'm sorry, I forgot to tell you. After the gunshot at Beacon's landing, I received a phone call from an unknown number. All the voice said was, 'Next time, you won't get away.'"

Justin sighed. "You should have told me."

"I know. But I couldn't identify the voice, either. I can't say whether it was Boyd's voice or not." She felt bad about the lapse. Isaac slipped his arm around her shoulders as if to reassure her.

"Sir? Is it possible Sullivan knew that Lieutenant Gomez has had a security detail escorting her anytime she's outside the ICU and decided to leave the brick and rose as a warning instead?" Sergeant Morris asked.

Three pairs of eyes swiveled to stare at the staff sergeant in surprise. The guy was roughly her age with dark hair and kind eyes, and she found herself impressed by his insight.

"It's possible," Justin acknowledged. "At this point, I'm open to any and all reasonable theories. Which reminds me, what about the ex-boyfriend you mentioned the other day? Maybe this is his work?"

"It's not Leo's style," she insisted.

Justin didn't look convinced. "In the meantime, let's get a tech out here to check for fingerprints or other evidence."

Vanessa knew that the likelihood of finding fingerprints on the brick or the smashed rose was slim to none, but understood it was part of the process. "Is it okay if I go home?"

Justin glanced at Isaac, then nodded. "Sure. We'll let you know when we're finished processing your vehicle."

"I'll take them, Captain," Sergeant Morris offered.

"That's good," Justin agreed. "When you're finished, I'll need your report."

"Yes, sir." Morris gestured toward his car, which was parked beneath one of the bright lights scattered across the lot. "This way."

Isaac dropped his arm from her shoulders, but reached for her hand. She clutched it tightly as they followed Morris to his vehicle. Isaac opened the front passenger door for her and dropped to one knee, bringing Beacon close.

"Friend," he said to Beacon, putting his hand on Vanessa's knee. "Friend."

Beacon sniffed her legs, then wagged his tail. She tentatively scratched his silky head, staying clear of his healing incision, glad that the animal accepted her touch.

"Good boy," Isaac praised. He rose, closed Vanessa's door then slid in behind her.

Morris started the car and drove toward the exit.

"I live off Webster, just past Viking," she said.

"Yes, ma'am."

She winced. "Please, just call me Vanessa."

The cop flashed a smile. "Okay."

"And I'm Isaac. No need to stand on formality at times like this."

Morris nodded. "I'm sorry about your car."

"Me, too." She glanced over her shoulder at Isaac. "Does Aiden know?"

"Yes, I was with him when you called. I left Tango behind. Your brother agreed to keep him for a while."

She was relieved to hear it, although she still didn't like the idea of Aiden being at her place alone. The cop posted at the front door hadn't prevented a break-in, or the additional attempts to harm her. Something had happened almost every day.

Fear threatened to close her throat, making it impossible to breathe. Every day.

Would it continue until he succeeded in killing her?

Ten minutes later, Sean pulled into her driveway. She pulled herself together, barely making it out of the jeep when the front door flew open and Aiden came rushing out.

"Nessa!" He greeted her with a hug. "I've been worried."

She returned her brother's hug, feeling the sting of tears in her eyes. Despite all the horrible things happening to her, there was one good thing to come out of all this. Aiden was acting like the kid brother he'd been before he was sent overseas.

"I'm fine," she assured him, subtly wiping her eyes. "Easy enough to fix a broken window."

"I know." Aiden stepped back, revealing Tango at his side.

"Need anything else?" Sean asked.

"No, but thanks again." She flashed him a smile as Isaac and Beacon came to stand beside her.

"I was glad to be there. Keep calling for escorts while you're at work," Sean cautioned. "Each and every time you leave the ICU."

"I will."

Sean offered a quick salute and climbed back into his car. The three of them walked inside, nodding at the cop at the door.

"Isaac, are you going to sleep on the sofa again?" Aiden asked.

She was touched by her brother's protectiveness. He'd come a long way from that first night he'd met Isaac, glaring at him with suspicion.

"I will if Vanessa doesn't mind."

The pressure of being exposed to nonstop danger had her nodding quickly. "I'd like that."

Isaac didn't hesitate. "Done."

"Good." Aiden seemed satisfied with the added layer of protection. "I'll keep the puppies and Tango in my room." He glanced around the interior. "We are definitely outnumbered by the dogs."

That made Vanessa smile. Right here, right now, she felt safe. "'We'? I'll have Eagle in my room, Beacon will stay out here with Isaac. You're the only one outnumbered by the dogs."

"I don't mind." Aiden picked up the box of puppies, his grin making him look young and carefree. He spoke to the puppies and to Tango as he disappeared into his room, shutting the door behind him.

Then she and Isaac were alone.

"He's really coming along," Isaac said, gazing thoughtfully at Aiden's door.

"He is," she agreed. "Fostering the puppies has done him a world of good."

"I'm sure being here with you helped some, too." Isaac took a step closer and her heart quickened with anticipation. She longed for his reassuring presence.

"You've given him an unofficial chance with Tango," she pointed out, tipping her head back so she could meet his gaze. "And without Tango, we wouldn't have found the pups. Let's call it a group effort."

"Yeah." Isaac reached up and pushed a strand of hair behind her ear. "I missed you today."

Her heart melted at his frank admission. "I missed you, too."

"And I hate that you're constantly in danger." He cupped her cheek, then bent down slowly, lightly brushing his lips against hers. The kiss was soft and fleeting, making her yearn for more.

"Good night, Vanessa," he murmured, stepping away.

Disappointment stabbed deep. She couldn't deny she was getting tired of Isaac's mixed messages. One minute he was holding her and kissing her, the next he was pulling away.

As she returned to her room, she tried to let

go of her fear and focus on the fact that they were attending church together in the morning.

Wasn't helping Isaac rediscover his faith more important than her feelings for him?

Of course, it was.

But the knowledge didn't help her sleep any better. Not until she closed her eyes and lifted her heart and hope to her Lord.

Please help me guide Isaac back to his faith and Your loving arms. If all we can have is friendship, help me to accept Your plan, Amen.

Why had he kissed her?

Isaac turned on the narrow sofa, wondering if he'd ever get a full night's sleep again. Beacon was home where he belonged. He'd finally fulfilled his promise to Jake. He should be satisfied, but he wasn't. Being close to Vanessa and keeping their relationship on strictly friendly terms was killing him.

He wasn't sure he could keep it up. He'd almost clutched her close and kissed her long and deep, the way he'd wanted.

Tomorrow was Sunday, and he wished he could renege on his agreement to attend church services with Vanessa and Aiden.

But that was yet another promise he refused to break.

His eyelids fluttered closed and almost instantly he was back in the cockpit of the chopper, the sound of gunfire deafening.

Mayday! Mayday? We're under fire!

Abruptly he awoke from the dream to see Beacon licking his face, his paws planted on his chest. His breath came in pants as his pulse thundered in his ears.

He'd hoped the nightmares wouldn't return now that Beacon was home but he'd been wrong. Beacon had helped, but he was forced to admit that the nightmares might never stop.

Swinging into a sitting position on the edge of the sofa, he scratched Beacon behind the ears, drawing strength from the animal's presence.

Good thing the top brass had agreed to honor Isaac's request to retire Beacon from active duty. Losing his handler and then being separated from Isaac had caused the dog to exhibit all kinds of bad behavior.

If only they could see Beacon now.

Isaac couldn't sleep, fearing the nightmare would return. Dawn brightened the horizon, so he padded into the kitchen to start a pot of coffee. As it brewed, he took Beacon outside, startling the cop at the door.

When Beacon finished his business, Isaac headed back inside and helped himself to a large mug of coffee. The caffeine helped clear the cobwebs from his brain.

Aiden got up first, yawning as he carried the box of puppies outside. Tango followed as if knowing it was his job to assist.

Isaac remained inside to cook eggs for breakfast, although they were cold by the time Vanessa emerged, a good thirty minutes later. She looked lovely and fresh after her shower, especially the way her dark hair framed her face. His mouth went dry as he noticed her short-sleeved, burned-orange sweater and a billowy flowered skirt.

"Wow," he managed. "You look amazing."

"Thanks," she murmured with a blush. Then her brow furrowed. "You look exhausted."

"Yeah, well, as usual I couldn't sleep." He tried to downplay the symptoms of PTSD, although he knew as a nurse Vanessa probably understood. Better than Amber had.

"All the more reason you should come to church services with us," she persisted.

Again, he hesitated, then reluctantly nodded. "I guess I better get home to change into something decent." Isaac glanced down at his battle-ready uniform with a grimace. He didn't have a lot of formal clothes, other than his dress blues.

She glanced at the clock on the wall. "You have plenty of time. No need to rush."

Maybe not, but he needed some distance from

her enticing honeysuckle scent or he might do something foolish like kiss her again.

She didn't need a guy like him, bogged down with nightmares and mood swings.

Isaac warmed the eggs in the microwave and set the plate before her. Vanessa bowed her head and clasped her hands. "Dear Lord, thank You for providing the food I'm about to eat. Please continue guiding me on Your chosen path, Amen."

He felt guilty for not praying before his meal, although it wasn't second nature to him, the way it was for Vanessa.

They discussed their plans, agreeing to meet thirty minutes before the service, allowing plenty of time for them to walk, since Vanessa's car still hadn't been released. Isaac had also placed a call to Justin, requesting a second cop to be stationed at the house in case there was another attempt to get to the puppies.

When she finished breakfast, he helped with the dishes before heading home with Beacon. He hoped the pastor was open to airmen bringing their dogs to church services.

He spent some time with Beacon, grateful the dog didn't show any hint of weakness from his injuries and appeared content to be there with him.

The feeling was mutual.

An hour later, Isaac was showered, shaved and wearing his crisp dress blues. He walked back down to Vanessa's, struck again by her beautiful smile as she came down the steps toward him. It wasn't easy to persuade Aiden to leave the puppies behind with Tango, even though it was only for a little over an hour, but he finally agreed. The cop stationed at the door accompanied them as a second cop arrived to watch the puppies.

As they approached the church, Isaac was relieved to see that a few of the other airmen had their dogs with them, too. At least he wouldn't look completely out of place. At the threshold of the building, Isaac noticed a tall, light brown–haired man cheerfully greeting people as they entered.

"Good morning, Pastor Harmon," Vanessa said when it was their turn to enter. "I'd like you to meet Captain Isaac Goddard and his K-9, Beacon."

Isaac held out his hand and the pastor shook it.

"Welcome to God's house, Isaac. May you find peace and serenity within your faith."

"Thanks." Isaac followed Vanessa and Aiden inside, grimacing as they went directly to the front of the church. As much as he would have preferred hovering in the back, he reluctantly slid in beside Vanessa.

Sitting there, he wasn't sure why he'd agreed to come. Because of the recurring nightmare? No, because he'd promised. He stared down at his hands, finding it difficult to accept God's will after suffering the terrible loss of his closest friend, Jake. Who knew if God really had a plan? Maybe they were all on their own to flounder or flourish.

Vanessa picked up a small hymnal, offering it to him. He shook his head.

Pastor Harmon seemed to be looking at him through the entire service, making him shift uncomfortably in his seat. Another reason he preferred sitting in the back and well out of sight.

Then the pastor said something that struck close to home. "'In him was life, and the life was the light of men. The light shines in the darkness, and the darkness has not overcome it.'"

Isaac looked up and caught Pastor Harmon's gaze, stunned at the gentle knowledge and understanding reflected there. Isaac gave the pastor a brief nod, realizing that what the Bible said was true.

He'd used Jake's death as a way to avoid the light, as an excuse to stay in the darkness. But God was the light and he should never, ever have turned away from the Lord.

A sense of joy swept over him, and he reached over and picked up one of the small hymnals.

When the choir broke into song, he joined in, his voice low and hoarse and rusty, yet true.

Vanessa wrapped her hand around his and he was suddenly glad she was with him.

For the first time since the horrible crash, he wondered if this moment, right now, really was part of God's plan.

If so, he would be an idiot to let her go.

The peace he'd gained in church offered a keen sense of hope. It didn't take long for them to leave the building, separating themselves from the crowd as they crossed Canyon Drive.

A dark pickup truck with tinted windows picked up speed as it headed toward them. "Look out!" Isaac shouted.

He released Beacon's leash to grab Vanessa and Aiden with each hand. The cop beside them turned to point his weapon toward the oncoming truck.

The sound of gunfire was deafening and sent him to his knees.

Mayday, Mayday! We are under fire... In a heartbeat he was sucked back into the nightmare of his crash.

THIRTEEN

The truck bounced up and over the curb, then crashed into a tree. Staring in horror as the events unfolded, Vanessa caught a glimpse of the driver, slumped over the wheel.

Boyd?

Her mouth went dry and she took a step toward the truck. "I have to check on him."

"Isaac? Are you okay?" Aiden's voice had her turning toward Isaac. He was on his knees, his hands cradling his head.

"Stay with him," she told her brother. "I'll be right back."

The cop who'd taken the shot accompanied her to the truck. Bracing herself, she peered inside, expecting to see Boyd. But it wasn't. The driver was a stranger to her, just like the other guy, the one who'd tried to steal the puppies, had been.

She released her pent-up breath. The guy didn't move, and there was quite a bit of blood covering his chest. She put her fingers to his neck to check for a pulse, but found nothing.

He was dead.

"I had to shoot, or he would have hit us," the cop said in a low tone.

"I know." She bowed her head for a moment, asking God to have mercy for the man who'd tried to kill them. Then she turned away, heading back to Isaac and Aiden.

Isaac was pale, but on his feet. "The driver?" he asked.

She shook her head. "He didn't make it."

"I'm sorry," Isaac whispered, drawing her into his arms for a hug.

She soaked in his warm strength.

The sound of sirens filled the air, and she was grateful help was on the way. It wouldn't take long for Justin Blackwood to find out about this, either.

"He was going to kill us," Aiden whispered. "Just like that kid in Afghanistan."

She belatedly realized that her brother could very well suffer a setback after this. The truck coming at them was eerily similar to what had happened to Aiden in Afghanistan. Isaac loosened his grip, realizing she wasn't going anywhere, and she quickly pulled Aiden close in a sisterly hug.

"I'm sorry, Aiden. This is my fault. I shouldn't have gone to church with you. I should have known better. Everywhere I go brings danger."

Her brother clutched her close for a long moment. "It's not your fault, Nessa. It's that stupid Boyd Sullivan."

Two Security Forces vehicles pulled up to flank the crashed truck. She lifted her tortured gaze to Isaac. "I need to get Aiden home."

"Soon," he promised. "We'll need to give our statements to the Security Forces first."

She couldn't bear to look at the truck, knowing the driver was dead. *Why, Lord? Why is this happening?*

There wasn't a good answer. She knew it was God's will, but at times like this, it was difficult to simply accept that and move on.

Captain Blackwood joined them a few minutes later, his face pale and grim as he surveyed the scene. "What happened?"

"The truck came at us out of nowhere," Isaac said. "The cop had no choice but to shoot."

A muscle ticked at the corner of Justin's jaw. "I understand, I'm not blaming him for protecting you. But is there anything else you can tell me? Did either of you recognize the driver?"

"No, but I can tell you he's not Boyd," Vanessa said. "Not that it matters, I'm sure Boyd was behind this attack, the same as the other attacks. And I don't think he'll stop until he kills me."

"That's not going to happen," Isaac said forcefully.

Brave words, and while she appreciated Isaac's promise, she was beginning to lose faith. Not in God, but that she'd escape Boyd's next attempt.

"We got a license plate. The vehicle doesn't belong to anyone on base," Justin said. "We'll put his fingerprints through the system, see what pops up."

"Another fall guy?" Isaac asked. "Just like the one who tried to steal the puppies?"

"That's my take on it," Justin agreed.

Vanessa shivered. Isaac moved closer and she gratefully leaned against him.

"By the way, we're finished with your car," Justin told her.

"Did you find any prints?"

"Unfortunately not." Justin glanced between them. "I also looked into Captain Turner's alibi for the time frame in question. He has a rock-solid alibi."

"Are you sure?" Isaac demanded. "For the entire twelve-hour shift Vanessa worked?"

"We were able to pinpoint the time frame on the surveillance cameras," Justin explained. "The video angle isn't great, but we can see a shadowy, bulky shape of someone wearing a dark hood and ski mask slamming the brick through the window at eighteen thirty, almost a full hour before she found it. We were able to verify that during that same time frame, Captain Turner was in the ER tending to a patient."

Vanessa wasn't surprised. "I told you it wasn't Leo's style."

"Yeah, well, our investigation has stalled once again. We know Boyd is the prime suspect but haven't found him on base."

"Probably because he's using other people to do his dirty work," Isaac said in a flat tone.

"Did anything come from following Rusty Morton?" Vanessa remembered how Gretchen Hill had mentioned the trainer's suspicious behavior.

"Not yet, but we're keeping an eye on him." Justin turned back to the truck. Two airmen had placed the driver's body on a stretcher. "This guy and his connection to Boyd is my priority now."

She understood and silently agreed.

"If Rusty isn't Boyd's accomplice," Isaac said thoughtfully, "he still might be the one who sold the dogs to the Olio crime syndicate."

Justin raised a brow. "You could be right about that. I'll check him out further once I'm finished here."

It was almost an hour later before they were

allowed to head home, escorted by yet another cop. Vanessa found it difficult to look the cop in the eye, knowing that being assigned to guard her was likely one of the most dangerous jobs on base these days.

No one was particularly hungry, but Vanessa made soup and sandwiches to keep herself from going crazy. Aiden immersed himself in caring for the puppies, and she hoped and prayed they'd allow him to find a measure of peace.

"Come, Beacon," Isaac said. The dog obediently crossed over to sit at his side. Isaac ran his fingers over Beacon's fur and she realized he was checking the dog for injuries.

"Is he okay?" she asked.

"Seems fine." Isaac glanced at her. "Better than you are."

She shrugged, unable to argue. This latest attempt to kill her had been the worst yet. "How old is Beacon?"

"He'll be seven at the end of the month, which is one of the reasons the top brass agreed he could retire from active duty." Isaac shrugged. "That was the first hurdle I faced in getting him home. The second was his bad behavior."

She frowned. "He's fine. I haven't seen any evidence of bad behavior."

"I did a video chat with my buddy Frank a few

months ago and Beacon went nuts. Frank mentioned they were struggling with his training."

"Maybe he missed you." She leaned forward to stroke the German shepherd's head. Eagle nudged his way between them, so she turned her attention to her K-9.

"Well, now that he's home, I'm sure your nightmares will go away once and for all."

Isaac's face shut down and he abruptly rose to his feet. "They haven't, and I've accepted the fact that they never will. Excuse me, but I need to get home." He strode through the house to the front door, with Beacon at his side.

She wanted to call out to him, to ask him to stay, but sensed there was no getting through to him.

Despite the cop stationed at her front door, the house felt incredibly empty after he was gone. She put a hand to her chest in an attempt to ease the ache that was building within.

She cared about Isaac, so very much.

Yet, she understood Isaac didn't share the same depth and breadth of her feelings. Despite the heated kisses and being sheltered in his warm embrace, she could tell he was holding himself back. Treating her as a close friend, nothing more.

Had he done something similar with his former girlfriend?

She tried to take comfort in the fact that

she'd helped him find his way back to attending church. Closing her eyes, she prayed that God would show Isaac the way to healing.

With or without her.

Isaac still didn't have a meeting with Justin to discuss his future, and with everything going on, his buddy likely wouldn't have time for a while yet. Maybe he should go all the way up to Lieutenant General Hall. After all, if the commander wouldn't support his attempt to transition into another role, there was no point in trying.

It being a Sunday, he made a mental note to call first thing in the morning. If there wasn't a place for him within the Air Force, he needed to start making other plans.

His future loomed empty and bleak, making the rest of the day drag by slowly. Keeping occupied with Beacon wasn't helping to keep him centered as much as he'd hoped.

It was humbling to realize how much he'd come to depend on Vanessa, too.

When his phone rang an hour later, his pulse jumped when he recognized her number. "Vanessa? Is something wrong?"

"No, but I need a favor."

Anything, he thought, but managed to hold his tongue. "What's up?"

"I was asked to come in tomorrow morning to

help cover a sick call," she said. "Being at work seems to be the safest place for me to be these days, so I agreed. They need me to work a full twelve-hour shift and Aiden has an appointment at fifteen thirty with Lieutenant Colonel Flintman. Can you swing by later in the afternoon to watch the puppies?"

"Of course." He was glad Aiden was going back to therapy. "Don't worry about a thing."

"Thanks, I appreciate it. I think Aiden was going to cancel his appointment if you couldn't help out."

"I'll be there."

"I'll let him know."

"Vanessa, I'll escort you to work in the morning, and I need you to promise you'll continue to ask for escorts each time you leave the ICU."

"No need for you to be here. Justin stopped by and I now have a full-time cop to take me where I need to go."

"I see." He didn't know what else to say.

"Good night, Isaac."

"Good night."

Once, he'd liked the peace and quiet of his small house, but after spending so much time with Vanessa, Aiden and the pups, he realized how lonely it was.

Was it possible he was turning another corner related to his emotional health issues? Going back to being a pilot wasn't an option, and if he went into the civilian world, he wasn't sure what he could do there, either.

That night, the nightmare returned. As before, Beacon woke him up before he crashed. He huddled with Beacon until almost four in the morning, when he finally fell into a dreamless sleep. Thankfully Aiden's doctor's appointment wasn't until late afternoon, giving him the opportunity to sleep in.

Still, it bothered him that the nightmare had resurfaced again so soon, especially after he had Beacon home. Two nights in a row. He tried not to dwell on it, but the reenlistment paperwork mocked him from the kitchen table as he made breakfast, which technically should have been lunch, and drank two cups of coffee.

He made the call to Lieutenant General Hall anyway, feeling the need to understand his options. Or lack thereof. Pulling himself together wasn't easy, but he wouldn't let Vanessa down.

At fourteen thirty he strode purposefully to Vanessa's house to take over Aiden's puppy-sitting duties. Aiden was glad to see him and quickly reviewed the puppy's routine. Isaac assured the young man he could handle it, and sent him off to his appointment.

The four pups, especially Denali and Smoky, were becoming rambunctious, rolling around and playing, nipping at his shoelaces. Shenandoah was the smallest and seemed content to curl in the crook of his arm. He could see why being around the puppies helped Aiden relax because he felt his own burdens slip away as he played with the adorable balls of fur.

Lieutenant General Hall surprised him by promptly returning his call. "Captain Goddard? I'd like to see you as soon as possible."

"Yes, sir. I should be able to get there by seventeen hundred hours, maybe sooner."

"I expect to see you at seventeen hundred hours, then." The tone in the commander's voice didn't invite room to negotiate.

"Yes, sir."

When the door banged open sixty minutes later, Isaac was ready to go, knowing it would take time for him to go home to change and then to get across base to the Base Command offices. When he caught a glimpse of Aiden's face, he frowned. "What's wrong?"

Vanessa's brother didn't answer, didn't look at Isaac or the puppies, but wordlessly disappeared into his bedroom, slamming the door shut behind him.

Isaac quickly set the box of puppies aside, to head over to Aiden's door. He knocked lightly, but there was no answer. He tried again, harder, then turned the handle and pushed it open.

Aiden sat on the floor in the corner of the room, holding his head in his hands and rocking back and forth, clearly agitated. He was mumbling under his breath, but Isaac couldn't figure out what he was saying.

"What happened? What's wrong?"

No answer.

Concerned, knowing he couldn't leave nor could he stay until the end of Vanessa's shift without disobeying a direct order, he pulled out his phone to call Vanessa. If anyone could figure out what had happened with Aiden, it was likely his sister.

"Hi, Isaac."

"Vanessa? You need to get home as soon as possible."

"Why?"

He swallowed hard. "Aiden needs you. Something has happened and he's regressed, badly."

"I'll be there as soon as possible. Please, Isaac, don't leave him alone until I get there, okay?"

"I won't, but hurry. I have a meeting with Lieutenant General Hall at seventeen hundred hours." He disconnected the call and returned to the kitchen. Maybe the puppies would help.

He couldn't imagine what had transpired to send the thriving young man reeling backward into a pit of despair.

FOURTEEN

Vanessa was taking care of what was now her fourth Tyraxal overdose patient when Isaac called. As much as she wanted to drop everything and rush to her brother's side, it wasn't quite that easy to leave work.

She couldn't abandon her two critically ill patients.

Bothered by both the latest overdose of Tyraxal and the news of her brother's severe regression, she continued caring for her patients while at the same time calling nurses from the upcoming shift to see if anyone would be willing to come in early to relieve her.

On the third phone call, she was relieved to hear that Second Lieutenant Shelly Arron was willing to start her shift early. Knowing Vanessa had someone on the way made it easier to concentrate on everything that needed to be done.

Her patient with the Tyraxal overdose wasn't nearly as critically ill as the previous patients had been, either because Carson Baker hadn't ingested as much Tyraxal or because he'd been found earlier—she couldn't say for sure.

Regardless, she silently thanked God for sparing this young airman first class's life. And it occurred to her that maybe, once the airman recovered, they might find out where he'd gotten the medication. From the brief history the ER doc had obtained, it appeared Airman First Class Carson Baker hadn't seen any combat.

So why had he been given PTSD medications?

She made a mental note to let Captain Blackwood know about this latest overdose, then quickly finished her charting just as her colleague Shelly walked in. Over the next fifteen minutes Vanessa provided detailed information on the two patients she was handing over to Shelly, and when she finished, she was about to head straight home, when something made her pause.

Picking up the phone at the nurses' station, she called Flintman's office. His receptionist answered.

"This is Vanessa Gomez, I really need to talk to Lieutenant Colonel Flintman as soon as possible."

"He's with a patient," the receptionist told her. "But he should be finished in about twenty minutes or so."

"Let him know I'll be there. Tell him it's about my brother, Aiden."

"I will," the woman promised.

Satisfied that she had a plan, she stepped away from the desk to use her personal phone to call Isaac. "How's Aiden?"

"He's in his room." Isaac's voice sounded grim. "Are you on your way? He won't talk to me about what happened in therapy. Worse, I brought in the box of puppies and he wouldn't even look at them."

Her stomach twisted painfully. "I don't understand. He was doing so well!"

"It could be a small thing that triggered a powerful flashback. That's how PTSD works. It's rarely logical or tangible."

She knew he was right, but the possible explanation didn't make her feel any better. Fighting a wave of despair, she sighed. "Tell him the puppies need him. That Master Sergeant Westley James won't let him keep them if he can't take care of them."

"Aren't you coming home?" Isaac asked. "He's pretty bad, Vanessa. He's sitting in the corner, rocking back and forth."

She closed her eyes, wishing the image wasn't so clear in her mind. "Listen, I'm going to head up to see Lieutenant Colonel Flintman. He's finishing up with a patient and I want to catch him before he leaves for the day."

"He can't give you details about Aiden's therapy," Isaac protested. "It's confidential."

"I know that," she agreed. "But Aiden gave Lieutenant Colonel Flintman permission to talk to me about his treatment plan. I don't need specifics, but there has to be some explanation as to what sent my brother over the edge during today's session."

Isaac let out a sigh. "I guess it can't hurt. How long will you be? I'm already running late for my meeting with the base commander."

Vanessa hated the idea of leaving her brother alone. "Can't you reschedule your appointment?"

"It was an order, Vanessa. I promise to return here as soon as possible."

"Yeah, okay." She didn't like it, but understood. "Go then. But do me a favor, leave Eagle with Aiden. Tell him to protect. Eagle will stand guard over Aiden and the puppies until I get home."

"Vanessa—" he started, but she cut him off.

"Just go. Right now, I have to get up to Flintman's office. I'll head home as soon as possible." She disconnected from the call, swallowing her frustration.

She'd been in the Air Force long enough to know that disobeying a direct order would result in a formal reprimand or worse. She tried to accept that Isaac needed to go, but there was a small part of her that felt he could have handled things better.

Seeing as he suffered from PTSD, too, she thought he'd be more understanding of Aiden's plight.

She gave herself a mental shake. Isaac wasn't important right now. Her brother was.

The psychiatrist had to have some idea of how to manage this new facet of Aiden's illness.

Because she couldn't stand watching her brother suffer.

Isaac was halfway down Canyon when he abruptly stopped in his tracks.

He couldn't do it. Leaving Aiden alone didn't feel right. Turning to head back the way he'd come, he pulled out his phone and called Base Command.

"Lieutenant General Hall's office."

"This is Captain Goddard. Please extend my apologies to the commander, unfortunately, I won't be able to make our meeting after all."

"Excuse me, Captain, but I believe the commander issued a direct order."

He winced. "Yes, I know. I would never disobey an order unless there was a very important reason. The mental health and well-being of a young airman is on the line. Aiden Gomez is in the middle of a flashback and cannot be left alone. I'm sorry."

"But—"

He disconnected the call, wondering if this was how his career was meant to end.

Quickening his pace, he shook off thoughts of his uncertain future and considered what he might say to break through the wall Aiden had built.

He knew what it was like to be trapped in a nightmare. He'd suffered several instances just like Aiden's. But he was puzzled by the impetus behind the kid's regression. What had triggered the setback? He'd told Vanessa that it could be anything, yet he found it odd that Aiden had reacted so negatively after he'd been doing so well.

The truck attack from yesterday? Could be. It wasn't unusual to see a delayed reaction. It was also possible that Aiden had witnessed something on the way home from the hospital. Sweeping his gaze over the area, he didn't see any sign of violence.

Maybe Aiden had spoken of the truck attack during his session. If so, it could be that Lieutenant Colonel Flintman inadvertently said something that had triggered a flashback.

The more Isaac considered that possibility,

the more he believed it. It was the only thing that made sense.

Boyd Sullivan's attempt to harm Vanessa was causing collateral damage. To Aiden and the others who'd gotten caught along the way. Two deaths for sure—the man who'd tried to steal the puppies, and the driver of the pickup truck.

So much death.

Did Boyd Sullivan know Vanessa had a younger brother? What if he turned his attention to Aiden?

Isaac broke into a run, reaching Vanessa's house in record time. The cop stationed outside the door looked surprised as he offered a salute.

He returned the gesture automatically. "Is Airman Gomez still inside?"

"Yes, sir."

"Good." He moved through the kitchen, feeling a sense of relief when he noticed Eagle was sitting tall at Aiden's door. Exactly the way Vanessa had said he would be.

"Good boy. Protect, Eagle," he said as he moved past into Aiden's room. The Doberman rose to his feet for a moment, sniffed around the room for a minute, then sat back down on his haunches.

Aiden was still rocking in the corner, oblivious to the puppies rolling and playing around him. Tango must have sensed Aiden's distress, because the golden retriever was stretched out on the floor beside Aiden, with his wide head pressed against Aiden's hip.

Isaac hesitated, then offered a silent prayer.

Lord, please help me find a way to get through to this troubled young man. Grant me and give me the strength and wisdom to help him, Amen.

Feeling slightly more confident, Isaac approached cautiously. "Hi, Aiden. I'm back and willing to listen if you're in the mood to talk."

The young man ignored him, keeping up his rhythmic rocking back and forth.

"I know what it's like to suffer a flashback like the one you're going through," Isaac went on. "Sometimes it was the littlest thing that set them off, too. I don't want you to feel bad if that happened to you."

Nothing.

"Aiden, did watching the truck attack bring this on? Or was it something else? You didn't see anyone on your way back from the hospital, did you?"

More silence.

"If you did see someone, please let me know. If Boyd Sullivan is around, we need to find him before he can harm anyone else."

Aiden stopped rocking for thirty seconds but didn't meet Isaac's gaze.

"You know what Sullivan looks like, don't

you?" Isaac pressed. Talking about Boyd Sullivan seemed to be causing a breakthrough. Was it possible Aiden had seen the Red Rose Killer? "You've seen pictures of Boyd, right?"

Aiden resumed his rocking, but the movements were slower now, as if the young man was indeed listening to what Isaac had to say.

His heart filled with hope that he was causing Aiden's hard barrier to crack, letting a bit of light through. But he needed to do more. He knew, more than anyone, how easy it was to build a wall to protect your mind. He racked his brain to find a way to breach Aiden's protective barrier.

"Vanessa saved him once," he went on, hoping that more discussion about Boyd Sullivan would bring Aiden back to the present. "Your sister has a kind and nurturing heart. She told me she came across Boyd when he was injured and helped him out. Apparently he didn't want to go to the hospital and risk getting in trouble for fighting, so she bandaged him up with her own personal first-aid kit."

Aiden stopped rocking for the second time, and Isaac found himself holding his breath, hoping and praying that he'd explain what had happened.

"She cares about you, Aiden, very much. In fact, she's taking the change in your condition so seriously, she headed back to the hospital to talk to Lieutenant Colonel Flintman."

Aiden's head shot up, meeting his gaze. "No." The word was hoarse, as if the young man's throat was sore from silent screams.

"Yes, she did," Isaac confirmed with a gentle smile. "But don't worry, Flintman won't discuss details of your sessions with her. She only wants advice on how to help you."

"No!" Aiden's voice was louder this time, startling the puppies playing on his lap.

Isaac frowned, trying to understand. "No, what? Talk to me, Aiden. Tell me what's wrong."

"Blood!" Aiden reached out to grasp Isaac's arm, gripping it tightly. "No! Get to Vanessa!"

He still didn't understand. "Was Boyd waiting for you outside the hospital? Is that what you're telling me? Boyd is hiding and waiting for Vanessa?"

Tango lifted his head and nudged Aiden. The young man instinctively put his arm around the golden's neck. "Flintman is a bad guy," he finally said.

"Flintman?" Isaac felt the blood drain out of his face as the puzzle pieces fell into place. "You saw blood in Flintman's office? Because he's a bad guy?"

Aiden nodded then buried his face against Tango's fur.

Isaac sprang to his feet. How much time had passed since Vanessa left to see Flintman?

Too much.

He put a leash on Eagle, grateful when the dog accompanied him without a problem. He headed to the door, pausing for a moment when he saw the cop standing there.

"You need to stay here and guard Airman Gomez and the puppies, understand?" he said. "That's an order."

"Yes, sir."

Without hesitation, he ran outside with Eagle keeping pace beside him, calling Blackwood as he went, hoping and praying he wasn't too late.

FIFTEEN

Vanessa was intercepted by Captain Leo Turner on her way to see Flintman.

"How dare you accuse me of attacking you?" He approached with blazing fury in his eyes. "I know you were upset about our breakup, but this is a new low, Vanessa."

She really wasn't in the mood for Leo's theatrics. Interesting how he'd acted sweet as pie the last time they had run into each other, even asking her to meet him for dinner. There must have been some underlying ulterior motive she couldn't possibly understand.

"I didn't." She stepped to the side to move past him.

He grabbed her arm, stopping her. "You sent the Security Forces after me!"

A frisson of fear darted down her spine. Was it possible Leo was behind the attacks on her? Had he said something to Aiden, causing her brother to regress? She couldn't understand what motive he'd have for trying to kill her.

Then again, she didn't understand much about Captain Leo Turner.

Steeling her resolve, she looked down at his hand around her arm, then back up at him, her gaze narrowing. "Let me go, Leo, or you'll have a good reason to be afraid of the Security Forces."

He met her gaze squarely, then reluctantly released her. "I don't appreciate you dragging my name through the mud. I can tell everyone is staring at me behind my back, and it's all because of you!"

She shook her head, amazed that Leo could be so self-centered. What on earth had she liked about him in the first place? Oh, he'd wooed her with sweet words and promises, but now she understood he was a jerk through and through.

Regardless, she didn't have time for this. It was already well past seventeen thirty and the hospital crowd was thinning out. Most of the people in leadership roles were gone for the day, and she needed to get to Flintman before he left, too. "In case you missed the news flash, I was attacked several times over the past week."

"And you told the cops you suspected me?" Leo asked with a sneer.

"No. I actually told them that kind of behavior

wasn't your style, but maybe I was wrong about that. You did just grab my arm."

His gaze darkened with anger.

She stared at his dark eyes, wondering if he was the guilty one. Stiffening her resolve, she went on, "Even if you didn't attack me, you know those pesky Security Forces guys, they tend to follow up on every possible lead." She tsk-tsked. "So sorry they bothered you, Leo, and since you had an alibi for the most recent incident, Captain Blackwood doesn't think you're involved."

"I'm not involved," Leo said between gritted teeth. "I never did anything to hurt you."

Except cheat on her, she thought, but whatever. None of that mattered anymore. She glanced at her watch again. "You're right, you didn't do anything to physically hurt me. Let's keep it that way, okay? I have to go."

This time, Leo didn't stop her as she headed down the hall, walking fast. When she reached the elevators, she grimaced and took the stairs instead in an effort to save time.

If she missed Lieutenant Colonel Flintman because of Leo's ridiculously bruised ego over being questioned by Blackwood, she would be so ticked.

The stairwell took her up to the fourth floor.

She was breathing heavily by then, inwardly annoyed at her failure to stay in shape.

When she headed down the hallway, she hesitated, realizing that this corridor was remarkably similar to the hallway from the night of her attack. The lights were set low, since it was after regular business hours. She shivered, battling a wave of apprehension as she remembered, all too clearly, the horror as strong fingers wrapped around her throat.

Maybe she should have called Security Forces to accompany her here to Flintman's office. But it was too late now.

"Give me strength, Lord," she whispered. Ignoring her fear, she quickened her pace so she didn't miss the chance to speak to Aiden's doctor.

The door to Flintman's office was closed. Worried that he'd already left, she knocked on the door and listened for sounds of activity from inside.

She didn't hear anything. Twisting the door handle, she was surprised it gave. Flintman must not have left yet for the evening, or surely the door would have been locked.

Stepping across the threshold, she entered a plush reception area. Flintman's usual administrative assistant wasn't seated at the desk, the woman she'd spoken to must have left for the day. No one was in the waiting room, either, and Flintman's office door was closed.

Did he have a patient in there? As a nurse, she knew that she couldn't just barge in and interrupt a private therapy session. She hesitated, thinking it was possible he was simply staying late to finish up some paperwork. Stepping quietly, she moved toward the door and pressed her ear against the wooden door, listening intently.

She didn't hear the sound of muted voices, but for all she knew, the office was soundproofed. She debated sitting down to wait for a bit, then realized how foolish that would be if Flintman wasn't even in there.

Gathering her courage, she sharply rapped her knuckles against the office door. After what seemed like forever, the door opened and the balding middle-aged doctor, wearing his dress uniform complete with the silver lieutenant colonel leaf on his collar, stood across from her. Flintman looked happy to see her, peering with anticipation from behind his thick glasses.

Catching a whiff of his stale aftershave, she wrinkled her nose, remembering the same icky scent the night of her attack. Her eyes widened in horror as the memory clicked. But before she could move, Lieutenant Colonel Flintman roughly grabbed her and pulled her inside his office, slamming the door behind her.

Then he reached into his pocket and pulled out a gun.

What? Vanessa couldn't believe what she was seeing. Clearly, Flintman was the one who'd attacked her a week ago. Was he responsible for all the attacks? Or had Boyd done some of them?

And why would Flintman target her in the first place?

"Well, well. I knew it was only a matter of time until you figured it all out," Flintman said, his tone conversational.

"Figure out what?" she asked, trying not to stare at the gun in his hand.

"You know," he admonished, as if she was being obtuse on purpose. "Tyraxal."

"T-Tyraxal?" she stuttered, wondering how long it would take Isaac to realize she was in danger.

Too long.

Even if Isaac finished with the commander and returned to Aiden, her brother was in no shape to talk about whatever he'd seen during his therapy appointment.

Or maybe it was more what Flintman had said to Aiden. Had the psychiatrist threatened to hurt Vanessa? Was that what had sent Aiden reeling backward? She kicked herself, belatedly understanding that the reason Aiden had been doing so well was because he had been skipping his appointments with Flintman.

Until she'd forced him to return.

Oh, Aiden, I'm so sorry. I had no idea. Please forgive me.

Flintman let out a harsh laugh. "You're too smart for your own good, Lieutenant," he said, waving the gun as he spoke.

She needed to stay sharp, to stall as long as possible. "You're selling Tyraxal prescriptions, aren't you? To the highest bidder."

His expression twisted with hate. "Not selling, providing, all because of a small mistake I made—going into debt while gambling. The Olio Crime Organization set me up with the bookie and things went well for a while, until I started to lose, badly. When I tried to get out, they threatened to go to the lieutenant general if I didn't cooperate as their drug supplier. In order to pay off my debt, I had to give them Tyraxal prescriptions. Don't you see? I'm in line for a promotion to full colonel and even if I wasn't, I can't afford to lose my pension!"

Blackmail? She hadn't even considered that possibility. Even so, she couldn't feel sorry for the man who'd callously caused so much suffering. "You violated your own medical ethics as a way to protect yourself?"

He scowled and took a step toward her. "Yes, I

did. I've given the government twenty-five years of my life. There's no way I'm going to stand by and watch everything I've worked for go down the drain. Besides, it's not my fault people are getting hooked on drugs. If not Tyraxal, it would be something else." He shrugged as if it didn't matter one way or another.

She shuddered with distaste.

"The people using the meds wanted more and more, so I had to get creative, making all kinds of aliases for patients so we wouldn't get flagged by the government."

She knew he was referring to the new federal regulations that closely monitored prescriptions for controlled substances. If he wasn't careful, his name would be flagged as a high prescriber in the system.

If someone bothered to look. If the people buying scripts used a variety of pharmacies, his name wouldn't be easily flagged.

Keep him talking.

"And then your so-called *patients* started dying," she said.

He waved the gun again, as if that was nothing more than a minor inconvenience. "Not that many at first. Regardless, once you left me that voice mail message, I knew you were standing in the way of me meeting my goal. I only needed a few more months to get my promotion and retire as a full colonel. I decided it was time to get rid of you. Conveniently, you were targeted by the Red Rose Killer, so I knew your death would be pinned on Sullivan."

She swallowed a wave of nausea, remembering the words he'd whispered in her ear. *Because you're in my way.* She shook off the memory, trying to stay focused. "Okay, fine, you wanted me out of the way, but why attack Aiden?"

Flintman's expression went cold. "He saw me meeting with my contact within the Olio Crime Organization and overheard us talking. I figured, since you left the voice mail that same day, that your brother might have told you what he'd heard."

Thinking back, she realized that the day she found the puppies was the same day Aiden had been huddled in the corner of the living room when she'd come home. No wonder he'd started canceling his appointments. She wished she would have left it alone, rather than forcing Aiden to return to see Flintman.

It hurt her to realize Aiden's latest regression was completely her fault. But this wasn't the time to wallow in remorse.

Keep him talking!

"What happened earlier this afternoon?"

Flintman shrugged. "My contact came in again, only this time, we argued. I wasn't happy that these overdose cases were showing up at Canyon. He was supposed to keep the scripts off base. It was part of our deal. I demanded to speak to his boss, but he took a swing at me, so I grabbed the paperweight off my desk and hit him in the head." He shrugged. "You know how much head wounds bleed. I didn't kill the guy. He left on his own two feet. But I didn't realize anyone was near, until I heard footsteps rushing out of the waiting area." His eyes gleamed with madness. "I knew then that Aiden had heard everything."

She knew Flintman was pathologically criminal and possibly insane. She could easily picture Aiden lingering after his appointment in order to hear what Flintman and his buyer were saying, until the assault and blood transported him back in time to when he'd witnessed his buddy's death from a suicide bomber.

Poor Aiden. None of this was his fault; it was all on her. Because she'd raised the alarm about Tyraxal.

She thrust her chin forward and put on a brave front. "You bashed in my car window as a warning, didn't you?"

He shrugged. "I wanted you to be afraid of being here at the hospital. You could have easily taken a leave of absence or something. But here you are."

"And the truck that tried to hit us? The shots outside the Winged Java? Did you arrange for those events, too?"

He smiled, and the tiny hairs on the back of her neck lifted in alarm. "It's amazing what some people will do for another prescription of Tyraxal, isn't it?"

She could barely stand to look at him. *Dear Lord, help me escape this evil man!*

"So now what? You're just going to shoot me here in your office? Talk about a stupid move. It won't take long for Captain Blackwood and his team to figure out the link between my death and Tyraxal. Especially because I've shared my suspicions about you with the team."

That information caught him off guard, and he took a threatening step toward her. "You told them about me?"

Stretching the truth didn't come easy, but her desperate situation required it. She scoffed, as if he was an idiot. "Of course. Why wouldn't I? You went overboard with all these attempts to harm me, so I had to tell Captain Blackwood everything, including my concerns about you using too much Tyraxal. Don't you see? Killing me will point the finger of guilt directly at you."

He stared at her for a long moment, then shook his head. "No way. If anyone within Security Forces knew you were here, they'd already be banging down my door. But thanks for the warning. It's time for us to get out of here." He leered at her. "And when I'm finished with you? Guess who the next victim of a Tyraxal overdose will be?"

No! Not Aiden! She tried to think of a way out of this mess. If only she hadn't left Eagle behind.

"Wait, one more question. Did you arrange for someone to try stealing the puppies from my house?"

Flintman nodded. "I convinced one of my prescription buyers to do the deed, promising to give him six months of Tyraxal for free. I wanted those puppies gone, since Aiden used them as an excuse to cancel his appointments with me. Too bad the moron got himself killed."

The way he'd tried to manipulate Aiden made her stomach burn with anger. The despicable man had attempted to hurt her brother worse than if he'd simply stabbed him.

"I tried to kill you and Aiden in one fell swoop using the truck to attack you, but after that failed, I knew I needed to take care of you myself. Thanks for calling to make an appointment with me. You really helped make things easy." He glanced around the office. "Enough talking. It's time for action."

Action? She dreaded the thought of leaving the hospital, fearing Isaac might never find her.

"Move. Now!" Flintman aimed the gun at her face. "Don't try anything stupid. We're going to walk out of here together."

She wasn't sure how to stall for more time. He'd admitted to most everything, but only because he planned to kill her and eventually Aiden, too. This man had violated his code of medical ethics all to protect his reputation, rank and retirement.

Not caring how many innocent lives he'd sacrificed along the way.

Please, Lord, help me! Give me Your strength and wisdom! Don't let this horrible man get away with cold-blooded murder!

Isaac and Eagle arrived at Flintman's office well before Justin or his team did. He hesitated, wondering if he should wait for backup, but overwhelming concern for Vanessa had him opening the door and stepping inside the plush office.

Loud voices from behind the door leading into Flintman's office indicated there was trouble. Isaac unleashed Eagle, knowing that the well-trained, protective K-9 was the only weapon he had.

He stepped toward Flintman's office door when it abruptly swung open, revealing Vanessa. For a fraction of a second her eyes widened in surprise, then she mouthed the word *gun* and abruptly dropped down to her knees.

"Attack!" Isaac ordered as he dove to the floor. Thankfully they seemed to catch Flintman off guard as Eagle went over and clamped his jaw around the man's right ankle with a low, fierce growl.

"Owww!" Flintman screamed, wildly waiving his gun. "Grab the dog off me! I'll shoot him! I'll shoot you all!"

Vanessa abruptly lunged to her feet, kicking Flintman directly in the left kneecap. He howled in pain and teetered precariously, attempting to maintain his balance. Isaac used the moment to rush forward and grab the guy's wrist, roughly twisting the gun from his hand.

Flintman cried out again then crumpled to the floor. Isaac tossed the weapon aside and jumped onto the prone figure of the doctor, pressing his face against the floor. "It's over, Flintman. You're a disgrace to your rank and profession."

"Too bad I missed when I took that shot at your stupid dog, Beacon," the doc muttered.

"What did you say?" Isaac was dumbfounded by the man's confession. Had Flintman really been the one to shoot at Beacon during the animal's homecoming? It hadn't been a shot meant for Vanessa?

"You heard me." The man struggled against

his weight. "Let me up! I'm hurt! I need medical help!"

"Why?" Isaac was truly bewildered by the psychiatrist's attempt to harm Beacon.

"You chased me off the night I tried to take care of Vanessa. After that, I thought if I got rid of the dog, you'd go into a deep pit of despair." Flintman flashed an evil smile.

Isaac was shocked by the news and understood that Flintman was likely responsible for everything that had transpired in the past week. None of it had been related to Boyd Sullivan.

Flintman continued wiggling beneath him. "Get off me! She broke my knee and the dog bit me! I demand to see a doctor!"

"Roll him over," Vanessa instructed, dropping down to her knees beside Flintman. "I need to take a look at his injuries."

Isaac reluctantly did as she requested. "One false move and I'll kick your other knee," he warned as he released his hold on the older man. "Eagle, guard."

The Doberman came over and sat right next to Flintman's head, showing his teeth. Vanessa smiled weakly, then leaned over to examine the man's injuries. "Does this hurt?" she asked as she gently palpated his swollen knee.

"Yes." Flintman peered up at her, his glasses sitting askew on his face. "I knew you cared."

"What?" Vanessa reared back, staring at Flintman as if shocked by his statement.

"Something wrong?" Isaac crouched beside her.

"Oh, no." She shook her head. "It's just that Boyd Sullivan said the exact same thing to me when I provided first aid to him in the dark alley all those years ago."

He nodded, still not understanding her reaction. But at that moment, the door to Flintman's office burst open. Justin and his K-9, Quinn, led the way inside, followed by other armed cops.

"You're late to the party," Isaac said, relieved that the danger was over. "I disarmed Flintman. His weapon is in the corner."

"I've got it," one of the cops announced as he carefully picked up the gun between two fingers and dropped it into an evidence bag.

"You'll want to test it for ballistics," Isaac said. "Flintman admitted he was the one who took a shot at Beacon at his homecoming. It's likely he was also the one who tried to shoot Vanessa at Winged Java."

"He was the one who attacked me, broke my car window, hired that guy to steal the puppies and hired the man who tried to run us over with a truck," Vanessa added. "All because I raised the alarm over the recent Tyraxal overdoses. Apparently, he's being blackmailed by the Olio

Crime Organization and as a result has been giving them Tyraxal prescriptions."

"Unbelievable," Justin muttered.

"Oh, and you might want to go through his office, too," Vanessa added. "He mentioned assaulting one of his contacts with a paperweight. He claims he didn't kill the guy, but the paperweight may still have trace evidence on it."

"We'll go over the place carefully," Justin assured her, his expression bleak.

Isaac understood that finding evidence against Flintman and arresting him for the recent events meant the Security Forces team was no closer to finding Boyd Sullivan.

For all they knew, Sullivan may not even be on base.

"I want a lawyer," Flintman said. "I'll give you evidence against the Olio Crime Organization if you'll cut me a deal."

The thought of Flintman getting a deal made Isaac furious, but he understood how the system worked. Besides, at this rate, the guy would be too old to be a threat by the time he got out of jail.

"Oh, don't worry, you'll get a lawyer." Blackwood stood over Flintman, looking down at the guy with disgust. "But don't pin your hopes on getting a deal. If I can link you to the recent overdoses, you'll be on trial for murder."

Flintman went pale at the threat, and Isaac nodded with satisfaction.

The immediate threat against Vanessa was over, but that only meant Boyd Sullivan was still out there, somewhere.

And there was no way to know the identity of his next victim.

SIXTEEN

Vanessa wanted nothing more than to get back home to check on Aiden, but she had to wait until Justin had finished taking her statement.

"I need to make sure I understand his motive," Justin said. "Did Flintman mention any details about why he was being blackmailed?"

She thought back to what he'd revealed. "He said he was set up by the Olio Crime Organization who encouraged him to gamble. He apparently won at first, then began to lose. When he got further into debt, they used that as a way to blackmail him. They threatened to end his career if he didn't pay them back by writing prescriptions of Tyraxal." It made her sick to her stomach to realize Flintman had saved himself at the expense of ruining young people's lives. "When I noticed the pattern of Tyraxal overdoses, he decided he had to eliminate me."

"Why go after your brother?" Isaac asked.

"Aiden overheard Flintman meeting with his

contact within the crime ring on the same day I left him the message about my concerns regarding the Tyraxal overdose." She swallowed against a tight ball of guilt. "Aiden did the right thing, putting distance between himself and Flintman by canceling his appointments. Until I forced him back."

"Vanessa," Isaac said, his voice low and husky, "it's not your fault. You had no way of knowing Flintman was being blackmailed into writing prescriptions for Tyraxal."

"No, I couldn't know that. But I should have left Aiden alone. He was doing so well after not seeing Flintman for several days, but now..." She let her voice trail off, battling back the sting of tears.

It was her fault and that was something she'd have to live with for the rest of her life. Who knew how long it would take Aiden to recover this time? Remembering how Isaac had said he was rocking in the corner, suffering so badly, the adorable puppies hadn't been able to break through his wall of despair.

She sent up a silent prayer that God would help Aiden find his way back to being healthy.

"Anything else?" Justin asked.

"Not that I can think of at the moment," she said. "If you don't mind, I'd like to see my brother now."

Justin nodded, glancing down at his K-9, Quinn. "That's fine. If I need anything more I'll let you know. My next job will be to pry information about the Olio Crime Organization from Flintman."

She wanted Flintman to be held responsible for the Tyraxal overdoses, as well as the multiple attacks on her, including the young cop's. And she especially wanted him to be held accountable for the way he'd attempted to destroy Aiden's mind, his very being.

It wouldn't be easy to forgive him for what he'd done to her, to other innocent people and to her brother. God would want her to try, and she would, but not yet. It was too soon. Not until she'd talked to Aiden for herself.

Her brother had already been through so much.

"Oh, one more thing," Justin said as she made her way to the doorway.

She glanced at him over his shoulder. "What?"

"Isaac mentioned that Flintman said something that triggered a memory about the night you helped Sullivan."

"Yes, that's true," she reluctantly agreed.

"Tell me what happened."

"When I knelt down to provide first aid to Flintman he said, 'I knew you cared.' Back when I treated Boyd, he said the same thing while trying to kiss my cheek. I instinctively shied away to avoid his kiss, and told Boyd that as a nurse, I cared about everyone. At the time, he seemed fine. He even thanked me for helping him out when no one else would."

Justin nodded thoughtfully. "Interesting. Looking back at Sullivan's pattern of killing those who rejected him, maybe he wasn't as okay with the way you avoided his kiss as he seemed."

She shook her head in amazement. "I assumed it was kind of a brotherly thing, because that's how I felt toward him. He reminded me of Aiden, of how I had to take care of my brother after our parents died." She knew that Aiden's decision to follow her into the Air Force had been made in part because he didn't want to be too far away from her. "It's crazy to think that shying away from him was enough to target me as a person to kill."

Justin's expression went hard. "Trust me, most of the so-called transgressions against Sullivan were nothing more than a word or action that hurt his pride. The interaction you just described explains why he sent you a red rose, despite the fact that you helped him out by offering first aid."

She felt foolish for not having mentioned the brief interaction sooner. "I'm sorry, but at the time, I didn't think much of it. But when Flint-man said the same thing, I instinctively shrank away, the same way I did that night with Boyd."

"It's not your fault, Vanessa," Isaac said again. "But at least now we understand what drove Sullivan to seek revenge against you."

It was incomprehensible to her that Boyd would send her a red rose just because she'd avoided his kiss. And if Boyd hadn't sent the stupid rose, Flintman wouldn't have had that threat to use as a cover for attacking her.

Her temple throbbed with the effort to think. She was exhausted, and her entire body felt as if she'd been battered by a group of ninja warriors. "I need to see Aiden."

"I'll take you home." Isaac handed her Eagle's leash and she took a moment to kneel beside the K-9, giving him a grateful hug for the role he played in saving her life.

She owed Isaac her gratitude, too.

She rose to her feet and followed Isaac out into the hallway. Isaac fell into step beside her, staying protectively close. Part of her wanted to lean on his strength and support, especially since he'd come running with Eagle to her rescue.

"Wait a minute. How did you know I was in trouble?" she abruptly asked, frowning in confusion.

Isaac waited for the elevator doors to open,

then ushered her inside, hitting the button that would take them to the main level. "I called and canceled my meeting with the commander, so I could head back to your place to continue talking to Aiden."

Had he really blown off a meeting with Base Commander Lieutenant General Hall?

"Oh, Isaac, I'll feel terrible if you get in trouble over this."

He shrugged, avoiding her gaze. "It was worth it."

She was touched by his change of heart, then glanced up at him in surprise. "Are you saying Aiden talked to you?"

"Not right away," Isaac said with a grimace. "I did all the talking, reassuring him that we'd be there to help him through this. I can't remember everything I said, except that when I mentioned how you had gone to talk to Flintman, his fear for your safety helped bring him back to the present. He mumbled about blood and then finally told me that Flintman was a bad man."

"Aiden actually said that?"

"Yes. He told me to get to you, to save you from Flintman." Isaac put his arm in front of the elevator door, letting her and Eagle step out first. "I called Justin as I ran here with Eagle."

"You ran?" she echoed in surprise. "I can't believe you beat Justin here."

"Part adrenaline and part God's strength," Isaac said as they walked outside. "I prayed the entire way."

Darkness had fallen and Vanessa couldn't stand the idea of her brother being home alone in the dark. She quickened her pace, heading straight for her SUV. She opened the back for Eagle, who knew the routine enough that he gracefully jumped in. She closed the hatch behind him.

"I'm thankful I made it in time," Isaac added, opening the passenger-side door for her.

"Me, too." She stood beside him, offering a wan smile. "Thank you, Isaac, for saving my life."

"Anytime," he said in a low voice. He gently pulled her close and she hugged him, resting her cheek against his broad chest.

She ached to kiss him but knew there wasn't time, so she reluctantly pulled away. "I'm sorry, but we need to hurry home. I can't bear the thought of Aiden being there with a cop he doesn't know."

"Of course." Isaac's expression was troubled, but he nodded, taking her car keys and sliding in behind the wheel. Surprised that he'd decided to drive, she sneaked a glance at his handsome profile, wondering if they'd drift apart now that she was no longer in imminent danger.

Sure, Boyd was out there, somewhere, but the recent attacks had all been Flintman's doing. Justin would no doubt get rid of the cop stationed outside her door, and honestly, she couldn't blame him.

No point in wasting resources that could be better used to track down Sullivan.

Isaac didn't say anything more as he drove her home. Plagued by a sense of urgency, she barely waited for him to stop the car before leaping out and rushing up the sidewalk past the cop at her door, to head inside.

She stumbled to a stop when she saw Aiden was sitting at the kitchen table holding Shenandoah in his arms, with Tango's head in his lap.

"Nessa!" Aiden staggered to his feet and lurched toward her. She hurried over to meet him, wrapping her arms around her brother's shoulders, making sure not to crush the puppy.

"Shh, it's okay. I'm safe, Aiden, and so are you. Lieutenant Colonel Flintman has been arrested by Captain Blackwood. I promise you, he won't hurt anyone again."

"I was so scared," her brother whispered hoarsely.

"I know, and I'm sorry." She loosened her grip so that she could look into her brother's dark eyes. "I never should have forced you into making another therapy appointment. I didn't know he was doing bad things, Aiden, or I wouldn't have made you go back. I was wrong, so very wrong. I should have trusted your judgment."

"My judgment hasn't been my strength this past month," Aiden said in a low voice. "I thought what I'd overheard was nothing more than another waking nightmare."

Her heart squeezed in her chest for everything he'd suffered. "Oh, Aiden. I'm so sorry for what that man did to you. Will you please forgive me?"

"Hey, there's nothing to forgive," her brother responded. He placed his free hand on Tango's head. "In fact, I'm relieved Flintman has been arrested. It helps knowing that I wasn't totally losing my mind. To know the heated argument and the blood was real."

She nodded, giving him another quick hug before stepping back and subtly wiping at her damp eyes. Eagle came to stand beside her, as if sensing her distress. She glanced at where Isaac stood near the doorway.

"Thanks again, Isaac. I appreciate everything you've done for me and Aiden."

He frowned. "Can we talk outside for a moment?"

She hesitated, glancing at Aiden. The way her brother had looped his arm around the golden's neck, pressing his face against Tango's soft fur, warmed her heart. Between Tango and the puppies, she firmly believed her brother would soon be back on the path to healing.

Although, it wouldn't be long before Westley would want to reunite the puppies with their mother, especially since she'd heard during her lunch break that the puppy's mother was doing better. No doubt he'd want to begin training the national parks as future K-9 military officers.

As she followed Isaac outside, she felt as if she knew what was coming. This was the goodbye speech. Isaac wouldn't need to stick around. In fact, she realized they'd never spoken about the future.

She knew she would be on base for at least the next year, since she'd already done a tour overseas.

What was Isaac planning to do?

She knew he'd been through a lot in Afghanistan, suffering the loss of his copilot, his best friend, then Beacon. It made sense that he'd offered to protect her as a way of making a difference.

She only wished their closeness over the past eight days had been built on something other than Isaac's desire to be needed.

That he cared about her the way she deeply cared about him.

Not just cared, but loved. She'd fallen in love with him.

No sense in worrying over things she couldn't change. Isaac would always be a good friend. Nothing more, nothing less.

It was time to say goodbye.

Isaac stood for a moment, waiting for Vanessa to join him on the sidewalk outside her house. When she came over to stand beside him, he noticed how the glow of moonlight bathed her skin.

Her beauty, inside and out, took his breath away.

"I'm sorry," he said, deciding to cut straight to the point.

She lifted a shoulder, shivering a bit in the cool night air. Vanessa hadn't changed out of her thin scrubs, and he had to battle the urge to once again pull her into his arms. "It's okay, I understand. Disobeying a direct order isn't something to take lightly."

"No, but it's not just that." He wasn't sure how to explain that he'd initiated the meeting.

That it was his future on the line.

Her smile was sad. "I really do understand, Isaac. It took me a while to realize just how important it is for you to keep the people around you safe from harm. Perfectly natural after everything you've been through during your last deployment."

Deployment? Now he was confused. "Everyone? Who is everyone?"

"Me and Aiden for starters. And I think there will likely be others. As soon as you find the next person who needs assistance, you'll be there to step up in the role of protector." She crossed her arms over her chest. "But obviously now that Flintman is under arrest, I don't need your protection anymore."

"You're not making sense," he muttered, wondering if his own fatigue and lack of sleep from the night before was getting to him. "It's not just about helping people, it's about having a future. A career. Don't you understand? PTSD will always be a part of my life."

She tipped her head to the side. "I'm a nurse, Isaac. I think that's one thing I do understand. But this isn't just about your illness. It's about something more. I believe you have a hero complex. A deep, desperate need to come to people's rescue."

"Hero complex?" he repeated, feeling stupid. "How about a guilt complex? My best friend is dead because of me!" His voice seemed overly loud even to his own ears, so he did his best to calm down. "I witnessed someone attacking you and wanted to keep you safe. All of this—" he swept his hand out encompassing the space around them "—is a way to atone for my sins."

"What sins, exactly?" Vanessa asked, her expression perplexed. "You were flying a chopper that was under fire by the enemy. Help me understand why that's your fault. What sin caused your buddy's death?"

A heavy pressure built in his chest, suffocating him. This was something he hadn't admitted to anyone. Not his therapist, not his CO. Not even himself.

Until now.

It was time he faced the truth, no matter how painful.

"Arrogance," he admitted. "My sin was arrogance."

She arched a brow, her expression skeptical. "I doubt it."

"It's true. I heard distant gunfire, and should have immediately gotten us out of there, but I waited too long." He tried to swallow but his throat felt as if he were being choked by a big black anaconda. "I thought I could steer the enemy in the wrong direction, before finding a way out of the tight spot we were in, the way I always had before. But that's not what happened. The chopper took a direct hit, I crashed and my copilot and Jake died." He was glad for the darkness that surrounded him when he added, "There were plenty of times I wished I'd died, too."

"But you didn't," she reminded him. "Beacon saved your life and you saved his in return. Not to mention the way you rushed to my rescue tonight. Don't you see? This is all part of the plan God had in store for you."

Was it? He wasn't convinced.

"God forgives us our sins," she went on. "Remember Pastor Harmon's service? When he spoke about walking in the light and forsaking the darkness, he meant we need to believe in God's word. To accept His truth. To follow His plan."

The tightness in his chest abruptly eased as the truth sank deep. A sense of calm swept over him, making him relax.

She was right. He would choose light over darkness. God's light.

"I'll try to remember that," he said.

"I'm glad. It means a lot to me that you found your way back to your faith and to God." Her expression softened and once again, he wanted nothing more than to pull her into his arms.

Yet everything that had transpired between them gave him pause.

It was time to be brutally honest with himself.

What sort of a future did he have to offer Vanessa? Especially now that he'd disobeyed a direct order from Lieutenant General Hall? No clue. He hadn't touched the reenlistment papers on his kitchen table. And if he did decide to sign them and turn them in, he couldn't avoid the possibility the Air Force would recommend a full physical that could easily end up with him facing a medical discharge based on his mental health issues.

He knew, better than most, that you couldn't have a pilot flying choppers while suffering PTSD. Driving Vanessa home tonight from the hospital had been the first time he'd been behind the wheel since Flintman fired a gun at Beacon, and he'd sweated every second of the short drive.

Despite the strides he'd made in the past few months, and being reunited with Beacon, he couldn't say that he was cured.

Quite the opposite.

There was no cure. Only a variety of strategies he could utilize in order to deal with his symptoms.

"Isaac?" Vanessa's voice brought him out of his thoughts. "Something wrong?"

"Nothing," he said, while thinking, *Everything*.

It was one thing to tell yourself to follow God's plan, but another to actually put the words into action. He could easily accept that God had saved his life, and Beacon's, for a reason. That he'd come back to Canyon to help Vanessa and Aiden.

But was that all God had in store for him? Probably not, but from where he was standing, his future still looked bleak and empty.

"Well, I guess I should go inside." Vanessa's voice broke into his thoughts.

He had no idea what to say, so he nodded. "I'll check in on you and Aiden tomorrow."

"I'm sure Aiden will appreciate that. I'm hoping he doesn't have nightmares over this." She hesitated, then added, "Good night, Isaac."

"Good night."

She disappeared inside, leaving him with the keen sense that whatever closeness they once shared was gone.

Possibly forever.

SEVENTEEN

Over the next forty-eight hours, Vanessa remained glued to Aiden's side, refusing to let him deal with his nightmares alone. Especially since Westley from the training center had called to let them know the mother was about to be discharged to Westley's care and it was time to reunite the mother with her pups.

Frankly, Aiden took the news better than she'd hoped, although he clearly didn't want to let go of Shenandoah, his favorite little runt of the litter. Putting on a brave face, Aiden accompanied her to the training center. As Aiden sat beside Tango and watched the mother sniff and lick her babies, she edged Westley aside for a personal conversation.

"I need two favors," she said in a quiet voice so Aiden couldn't overhear.

He grimaced. "Okay, but no guarantees."

"Isaac doesn't need Tango anymore now that Beacon is home." She gestured to the way

Aiden sat with his arm looped around the golden's neck. "Look at how Tango and Aiden have bonded. Don't you think they're the perfect match? I know he's failed one pairing, but this one looks promising. I'm hoping you'll give them a chance."

Westley nodded slowly. "Yeah, I can see that. Okay, sure, I can approve switching Tango from Goddard's therapy dog to Aiden's. I'll submit the paperwork right away."

"Thank you." She'd sailed over the first hurdle, but the second one was higher and far more difficult. "I know you're planning to train the puppies as future military dogs, and I'd like you to consider allowing Aiden to assist."

The master sergeant was shaking his head no, before she'd finished her sentence. "He doesn't have any experience with dog training," Westley protested.

"I know," she agreed. "But you said how impressed you were with the amazing job he did fostering the puppies. Notice how attached he is to Shenandoah?"

Westley didn't answer but watched her brother for a long moment.

"Aiden needs a purpose, something to look forward to. It's not fair for him to end up booted out of the Air Force because he's struggling with the aftermath of a suicide bomber that killed his best friend." She smiled as the four national parks fell all over themselves in excitement at seeing their mother. "He can start at the bottom, Westley, cleaning kennels, feeding and watering the dogs, or whatever. But please, please consider giving him this opportunity. I truly believe this is his calling."

Westley let out a sigh and stood watching her brother for several minutes. The puppies ran back and forth between Aiden and their mother, clearly exuberant. Shenandoah, in particular, lingered by Aiden's side. He gently lifted the puppy, nuzzled her for a moment then gently urged her toward her mother.

She held her breath, waiting, hoping, praying.

"Yeah, okay," Westley relented. "I'll take Aiden under my wing, assign him to work with the kennel manager, but he better not balk at the manual labor because I can promise that cleaning kennels is definitely part of the job description."

"He won't. Thank you," she whispered. "This means the world to me. To us."

"He has a connection to the pups already, so if all goes well, involving him in the pups' training helps me, too."

Training? She threw her arms around Westley in a quick hug. "You're awesome."

He shuffled about, looking uncomfortable yet pleased. "Yeah, yeah. That's what Felicity says."

Vanessa chuckled, but then experienced a sense of sadness. She remembered seeing Westley and his wife, Felicity, together on base and realized that's what she wanted. The closeness of a partnership, of leaning on each other, drawing strength from their love.

But Leo had been a complete and total jerk, and Isaac... Her chest tightened. Isaac was still wrestling with his own issues.

She hadn't heard from him, and doubted she would. Hopefully she'd see him at church services this next weekend. The only solace she had about everything that had transpired between them was that he'd embraced his faith.

She was happy to have had a small role in that reunion.

And if that was the only role God wanted her to have in Isaac's life, so be it.

She'd find a way to get over him, no matter how much it hurt.

Staying away from Vanessa wasn't easy, but Isaac couldn't in good conscience go see her when he didn't know what his future held.

Lieutenant General Hall hadn't been pleased with his canceling the meeting, but thankfully hadn't taken formal action against him. Isaac hoped that didn't mean his career in the Air Force was already over.

Instead, Isaac had tried to meet up with Justin for a personal, off-the-record discussion. Today, Justin returned his call, saying he was heading home for the day, inviting Isaac to meet him at his place at noon.

Isaac didn't need to be asked twice. He took Beacon with him and picked up a pizza along the way.

"Thanks for the grub," Justin said, pulling paper plates out of the cupboard. "Looks good."

"It does." Isaac was amazed at how much his appetite had improved over the past ten days.

Since meeting Vanessa.

As much as he hated to admit it, her claim that he was looking to rescue women wasn't entirely untrue. For the past eight years he'd been a battle-tested combat pilot. Now that he was grounded, it was no surprise that he needed something else to focus on.

But just because he felt better having something constructive to do didn't mean he didn't have feelings for Vanessa. She was wrong about that.

The problem was that he cared about Vanessa. Too much. His feelings for her were deep and complicated. He admired her strength, her intelligence, her dedication to her brother and to her patients. Even her stubborn nature. When he'd understood how much danger she was in, he knew that his life would never be the same without her.

Because he loved her.

"Isaac?" Justin's voice snapped him from his pensive thoughts. "You claimed you had something important to talk to me about."

He finished his helping of pizza and nodded. "I need career advice."

Justin's expression turned solemn. "Okay, shoot."

"I received my reenlistment paperwork and I'm not sure what to do. I doubt I'll be medically cleared to fly combat anymore. The risk of suffering flashbacks after my last crash is too great. I need something else to do."

"I see." Justin nodded thoughtfully, leaning his elbows on the table. "What are you considering?"

He stared at Justin for a long moment. "Don't laugh," he warned, "but I'm seriously considering a career in intelligence."

Justin's eyebrows levered up. "You mean Security Forces intelligence?"

Isaac nodded. "Exactly."

"Okaaay," Justin said slowly. "But if you want me to be honest, I need to tell you it won't be an easy transition. Most of our Security Forces candidates aren't coming in at entry level with the rank of Captain. I'm not sure that will fly with the brass."

"I know, and I'm willing to give up pay and accept a demotion if it means I have a career I'm proud of." Isaac spread his hands. "I don't want to leave the Air Force, and I think that I have something to offer by way of intelligence work. I was leaning that way when I first entered the Academy, remember?"

"I do," Justin agreed. "I was a year or two ahead of you but remember how they discovered your gift of flying and steered you toward being a pilot. After that, we went our separate ways."

"And here we are now," Isaac said with a smile. He wiped his damp, nervous palms against his BDUs. "Do you have any advice on how I should approach this with Lieutenant General Hall?" Isaac rose to his feet and began clearing the table.

"Why don't you let me talk to him first?" Justin suggested. "Considering your service record, I think I can convince him to grant you special dispensation to transfer without a demotion."

"Really?" Isaac tried not to get too excited about the possibility, but he couldn't help thinking that with Justin on his side, he stood a good chance at being accepted for a career transition. "I'd really appreciate anything you can do."

"Hey, what are friends for?" Justin asked. His phone rang, and he frowned at the number. "I have to take this. Rusty Morton is missing, can you believe it? Your instincts were right on target. He was most likely the one who sold four of our dogs to the Olio crime syndicate and now he's missing. Give me a minute, okay?"

"Sure." Isaac moved out of the kitchen, wandering down the hall as he attempted to give Justin the privacy he needed. He wondered how things were going with Justin's teenage daughter, Portia. As a single dad, Isaac knew that his buddy didn't have it easy raising a teenage daughter, especially since he hadn't been very involved in her life at the beginning.

Between being the captain of the Security Forces in charge of finding Boyd Sullivan and being a dad to a troubled teenager, Isaac wasn't sure which role was more difficult.

But he suspected the latter.

He glanced in her room, inwardly grimacing at the mess. Clothes were strewn everywhere, including her unmade bed. He imagined the chaos in here drove Justin crazy.

The glimpse of a red rose caught his eye, and he frowned, moving farther into the room. A red rose was taped to the frame of the laptop sitting open on Portia's desk, the only surface that was relatively clean.

What on earth?

Beneath the rose was a white note card. Printed in black where the words: *I'm coming for you.*

"Justin!" Isaac shouted to his buddy, while standing rooted to the spot, unwilling to tamper with evidence. "Get in here now!"

"What?" Justin sounded annoyed until he joined Isaac. Seeing the red rose and the note, he paled. "Sullivan was here? How? Why?"

"I don't know, but I think the computer is part of the message." Isaac nudged the mouse with the side of his hand. The screen flickered on, showing a half-finished anonymous blog post railing once again at the stupidity of the Red Rose Killer.

"What?" Justin's face went starkly pale as he lifted a trembling hand toward the note. "Portia? My daughter is the anonymous blogger?"

"Easy," Isaac said, putting his hand on Justin's arm. "I'm sure she didn't mean any harm."

"She's been leaking information for months!" Justin's pale face flushed red. "Things she must have overheard from me! I can't believe it. My own daughter!"

Isaac tightened his grip on his buddy's arm. "This isn't the time to be angry."

"You're right! This note means Sullivan knows Portia is the blogger. She's his next target!" Justin looked panicked. "I need to pick her up at school now! Before he can find her!"

"Go," Isaac agreed. "I'll wait here for the crime scene techs."

Justin was already calling in the team as he left the house. Isaac was shocked and stunned to learn that Justin's own daughter was the anonymous blogger. She'd leaked information, no doubt hearing tidbits of the investigation from her father, but it was her most recent post that worried him. The one that had almost taunted Sullivan, calling him a fool and worse.

Isaac sent up a silent prayer for his buddy and his troubled daughter.

The crime scene was processed with amazing efficiency, no doubt because no one wanted to risk their Captain's wrath. The idea of Justin's daughter being the next target for Sullivan was enough to keep every cop on their toes.

When the crime scene was secure, and Justin had returned with Portia, Isaac left. He stopped at home long enough to complete his reenlistment paperwork and submit it to Base Command, feeling good about the possibility of a new career, especially since Justin had offered his assistance.

And he made another phone call to Lieutenant General Hall, begging for a second chance. He was surprised and grateful when the base commander agreed to another meeting first thing in the morning.

Feeling better about his future, he sat for a moment, contemplating his next step. Thinking back over his relationship with Vanessa, he felt as if the kisses they'd shared were promising.

He needed to convince her that he wasn't a hero, but a man determined to do better with his life moving forward.

With her.

He picked up his grandmother's heirloom and tucked it into his pocket. Maybe he was rushing things, but he needed her to know his feelings for her were serious.

As he approached Vanessa's house, it was odd not to see the familiar cop stationed outside her door. He understood that Flintman was behind bars awaiting his court-martial, but also knew that Sullivan was still on the loose. And the guy was obviously on base, considering the note and rose he'd left for Justin's daughter.

He knocked at the door, waiting patiently for Vanessa. She answered the door wearing casual clothes—jeans and a gold sweater that complemented her golden skin.

"Isaac." She looked surprised to see him. "Is something wrong?"

"I—uh, wondered if you wanted to get a bite to eat. Maybe at La Taquiera." He felt like an awkward teen asking the prettiest cheerleader to go to prom. "If you're not fond of Mexican, we can go to Carmen's. The atmosphere there is a little nicer."

"Oh, sorry, Isaac, but I already picked up burgers for me and Aiden," she said. "We just finished eating. There aren't any leftovers, or I'd offer them to you."

He couldn't tell if she was avoiding him on purpose, or if it was nothing more than his rotten timing. What did it matter? He wasn't leaving, not like this. "Do you have time to talk?"

She glanced over her shoulder, then reluctantly opened the door and stepped outside. "I want to thank you again for giving up Tango. Westley has agreed to transfer him to Aiden as his therapy dog. The two of them have seriously bonded."

"I'm glad," he said, pleased that he'd been able to help. "What about the puppies?"

"Westley reunited them with their mother, and they're doing amazingly well. He's agreed to allow Aiden to help with training."

"That's incredible news," he said, even though he hadn't come here to talk about Aiden. He'd come to talk about them.

Specifically, the two of them together.

"It is," Vanessa agreed. "Aiden is thrilled to know that once he's cleared from medical leave, he'll be able to see the puppies every day, and between his new role at the training center and Tango, he's doing much better." She met his gaze head-on. "Thanks to you, Isaac. I want you to know how grateful I am for everything that you've done for us."

"You're welcome, but I don't want your gratitude." He searched her gaze, trying to gauge what she was thinking. "You accused me of having a hero complex, and maybe to some extent that was true. I'm a lot like Aiden, battling my emotional issues while searching for the key to my future."

Her expression softened and she reached out to rest her hand on his arm. "Oh, Isaac, I'm sorry. Surely you have a future here in the Air Force. The top brass would be foolish to let someone with your skills and reputation go."

He covered her hand with his, reveling in the softness of her skin. "Maybe. I've asked Justin for his support. I'm hoping to transition to working intelligence within Security Forces here on base. I even have another meeting with Lieutenant General Hall in the morning."

"Really?" Her eyes lit up. "That's fantastic."

He nodded. "To be honest, not knowing anything about my future was difficult. My PTSD symptoms have limited my options. I needed to have at least a plan of some sort before coming over here."

Her expression was full of chagrin. "I understand."

"Good. Because I need to make something perfectly clear. My feelings for you don't have anything to do with my so-called hero complex and need to protect you because I couldn't save Jake. I care about you, Vanessa. Very much. So much that being away from you over the past few days has been torture."

She hesitated, then smiled. "It's been hard for me, too," she confided. "I missed having you around."

His heart swelled with hope. "Vanessa, I know you deserve someone better, someone without the baggage that I'm carrying around, but I love you."

Her eyes widened. "Love?" she echoed hoarsely.

"Love," he repeated firmly. He took her hand and tugged her toward him. She readily walked into his embrace and as he hugged her close, he felt complete. He pressed a kiss to her temple, filling his head with her honeysuckle scent, then said, "I know you'll need time to assimilate this, but I'm begging you to give me a chance. I truly believe God's plan is for us to be together."

"Oh, Isaac." She tipped her head back, her gaze quizzical. "Are you sure? So much has happened—"

"I'm sure," he cut in. "More certain about how I feel toward you than anything else. I promise I'll never hurt you, cheat on you or lie to you. I love you, Vanessa." He swallowed hard, trying not to overreact. "Please give me a chance to show you how important you are to me."

"Yes." A broad smile bloomed on her face and she wrapped her arms around his neck. "I'll give you a chance if you grant me one in return. Because I love you, too, Isaac."

He sealed their agreement with a long, deep kiss that left them both breathless. He continued to hold her close, unwilling to let her go.

"We should probably tell Aiden, don't you think?" Vanessa asked, breaking their intimate cocoon of silence.

"In a minute." He eased away and took a deep breath, sensing the time was right. Subtly reaching into his pocket, he removed his grandmother's dainty engagement ring. An heirloom, the one that his mother had passed down to him before her death.

Holding Vanessa's hand in his, he dropped to one knee and presented her with the intricate gold ring. "Vanessa Marie Gomez, will you do me the honor of becoming my wife? This ring belonged to my grandmother, but if you don't care for it, I'm happy to replace it with whatever you choose."

"Yes! Yes, I'll marry you, Isaac." Her hand trembled as he slipped the ring on the fourth finger of her left hand. She stared at the ring with awe. "It's beautiful and fits perfectly. I'm humbled you chose to give me your grandmother's ring and I promise to cherish it forever."

"You deserve it." He stood and caught her close, swinging her in a circle as she laughed. "That and more."

"I deserve you," she said, going up on her tippy-toes to kiss him. "We deserve each other."

He couldn't disagree. The bright October sun rippled off the red, yellow and gold leaves on the trees, showcasing God's beauty.

In that moment, he knew he didn't have to worry too much about his future. Nothing else mattered but this moment.

They were blessed. Blessed with faith and God's love.

* * * * *

*The hunt for the Red Rose Killer continues.
Look for the next exciting stories in the
Military K-9 Unit series.*

Dear Reader,

I'm truly blessed to have been asked to participate in this latest Military K-9 series with such amazing authors. This was an amazing group effort. We laughed and we cried and I hope you agree that this is our best series yet.

I deeply respect the brave men and women who serve our country, especially those who have made the ultimate sacrifice in order to protect our freedom. Words cannot express my sympathy for those loved ones who have been left behind.

Researching this book was hard work yet also extremely informative and rewarding. While I have done my best to stay true to military protocol, please know that any transgressions are my own and were done only for the sake of the story.

I hope you enjoy Isaac and Vanessa's journey as they battle through danger and struggle with their faith in order to find everlasting love.

I love hearing from my readers, so if you have a spare moment, drop me a note or join my newsletter list through my website at www.

laurascottbooks.com. I can also be found on Facebook at laurascottbooks and on Twitter @laurascottbooks.

Yours in faith,
Laura Scott

Get 4 FREE REWARDS!

We'll send you 2 FREE Books <u>plus</u> 2 FREE Mystery Gifts.

Counting on the Cowboy
Shannon Taylor Vannatter

Reunited by a Secret Child
Leigh Bale

Love Inspired® books feature contemporary inspirational romances with Christian characters facing the challenges of life and love.

FREE
Value Over
$20

HOME on the RANCH

YES! Please send me the **Home on the Ranch Collection** in Larger Print. This collection begins with 3 FREE books and 2 FREE gifts in the first shipment. Along with my 3 free books, I'll also get the next 4 books from the Home on the Ranch Collection, in LARGER PRINT, which I may either return and owe nothing, or keep for the low price of $5.24 U.S./ $5.89 CDN each plus $2.99 for shipping and handling per shipment*. If I decide to continue, about once a month for 8 months I will get 6 or 7 more books, but will only need to pay for 4. That means 2 or 3 books in every shipment will be FREE! If I decide to keep the entire collection, I'll have paid for only 32 books because 19 books are FREE! I understand that accepting the 3 free books and gifts places me under no obligation to buy anything. I can always return a shipment and cancel at any time. My free books and gifts are mine to keep no matter what I decide.

268 HCN 3760 468 HCN 3760

Name _____ (PLEASE PRINT) _____

Address _____ Apt. # _____

City _____ State/Prov. _____ Zip/Postal Code _____

Signature (if under 18, a parent or guardian must sign)

Mail to the **Reader Service:**

IN U.S.A.: P.O. Box 1341, Buffalo, New York 14240-8531
IN CANADA: P.O. Box 603, Fort Erie, Ontario L2A 5X3

* Terms and prices subject to change without notice. Prices do not include applicable taxes. Sales tax applicable in NY. Canadian residents will be charged applicable taxes. This offer is limited to one order per household. All orders subject to approval. Credit or debit balances in a customer's account(s) may be offset by any other outstanding balance owed by or to the customer. Please allow 3 to 4 weeks for delivery. Offer available while quantities last. Offer not available to Quebec residents.

HRCBPA18R

READERSERVICE.COM

Manage your account online!

- Review your order history
- Manage your payments
- Update your address

> *We've designed the
> Reader Service website
> just for you.*

Enjoy all the features!

- Discover new series available to you, and read excerpts from any series.
- Respond to mailings and special monthly offers.
- Browse the Bonus Bucks catalog and online-only exculsives.
- Share your feedback.

Visit us at:
ReaderService.com